Wall of Silver

A Treasure Hunter's Dream

Written By
Richard Kellogg

Avery Color Studios, Inc.
Gwinn, Michigan

©2004 Avery Color Studios, Inc.

ISBN 1-892384-28-0

Library of Congress Control Number: 2004110606

First Edition 2004, Reprinted 2005

Published by
Avery Color Studios, Inc.
Gwinn, Michigan 49841

Proudly Printed In Michigan, U.S.A.

Disclaimer

Avery Color Studios, Inc., has published this book without representations or warranties as to the factual accuracy of its contents. The content of this publication is the literary expression of the author and is intended for entertainment purposes only. The sites described herein are on PRIVATE PROPERTY. Trespass upon private property may result in adverse legal consequences, including criminal and/or civil sanctions.

Neither Avery Color Studios, Inc., nor the author encourage, endorse, or sanction any activity or action taken to locate the property or places referenced in this publication, and neither the publisher nor the author shall be liable for any damages arising out of or in connection therewith.

Avery Color Studios, Inc.

Had news of this discovery reached England, our country might not have been born.

To The Adventurer

Clues within the story can lead you to close proximity of the lost mine. As Jake Stockard said, "Look for flaws in nature that man created."

Dedication

*In memory of my wife and best friend,
Barbara. 1931-1991*

Acknowledgements

My thanks to Michigan Technological University Mining Professor, Vernon B. Watwood for educating me on early mining and my dear friend Valerie for her inspiration. Further thanks to Matt Sutherland, who helped me begin my telling of history and to Avery Color Studios, Inc. for agreeing to publish my story.

Richard Kellogg

Thirty years ago I promised a friend that I would write a book about his discovery of an abandoned silver mine in the Keweenaw Peninsula, possibly the legendary "mother lode." This is mostly his story, but it became my story. Indeed it is a "story," not meant to be accepted as a historical record. The names of my contemporaries have been changed, but not my own. Sabin Stone and his contemporaries of the 18th century retain their actual names. Tragically many of the documents I used as background for this book were destroyed in a personal disaster. I believe I am the last living person to have seen the "Wall of Silver" mine. I hope I live to hear of its rediscovery.

Preface

In modern times, when most treasures have already been found, there still exists one waiting to be discovered. It is not in a remote jungle or in the unseen depths of an ocean; it is close to man. Found in 1927, in Michigan's rugged Keweenaw Peninsula, was a lost silver mine, its silver so rich and vast it might well be the much sought-after "Mother Lode" of the region. Proof of this cannot be found on a map. Its untapped wealth went undiscovered for more than 150 years, buried beneath rock and time.

Table of Contents

Introduction

A part of American History is missing. This story tells how close we came to not having our country born. It all began during the 1760s and 1770s. England was at war with France over the Northern Territory of the United States and Canada. At stake was their lucrative fur trade. In an effort to control the free world, England suddenly found its treasury nearly depleted. When word reached General Gage, commander of all British Forces in North America, from an outpost in the Upper Great Lakes Region that Indians were seen wearing trinkets of gold and silver, he sent word to England of the sightings. When word reached England, it caused such an uproar that Parliament went into a special session and decided that an expedition be formed to search for precious metals in the Upper Great Lakes Region. According to historical records the expedition was a failure. What history did not record is what happened to geologist Sabin Stone and the seven miners of that expedition. All we know is that Alexander Henry left the expedition at the Sault and reported to General Gage that they found

Wall of Silver

nothing in precious metals but large amounts of nearly worthless copper. From the journals of Sabin Stone that were passed down through generations, it is now known that, after Henry left the expedition, Stone stayed on at the Sault and did indeed find a rich lode of silver in the Keweenaw Peninsula. Word of his discovery never reached General Gage as he intended. Had the mine been put into production there may not have been the United States of America, as we know it today. Some 150 years later, a lone, unemployed geologist, Jake Stockard, on a cold day in the spring of 1927 discovered the lost mine that eventually made him independently wealthy. Stockard, before he died in 1971, passed on this incredible story to the author. Even after nearly forty years have passed, I find it most compelling to tell what he discovered in the lost Wall of Silver mine and the profound effect it had on his life.

Keweenaw
County

Map of the Midwest showing location of
Keweenaw County in Upper Michigan.

The Discovery

The price of copper is at an all-time low; the copper mines in Michigan's Upper Peninsula are shutting down. Unemployment is rampant, near-starving people are taking to the streets. Better off than most, unemployed geologist Jake Stockard, fearful of depleting his dwindling savings, decides to go prospecting. Already established as having a much sought-after rock and mineral collection and known for selling rare rocks and minerals to the many rich mine owners in the area, he packs his prospecting gear into his pickup truck and heads for the remote and rugged Greenstone Cliff Region. For hours he wanders the base of the cliffs searching the latest rockslides for new rocks and minerals. Finding nothing of value, he decides to set up camp and spend the night. While he is gathering wood for a campfire, his eyes catch sight of a sparkling stone; he picks it up; it feels heavy to his touch. Curious, he scratches its surface with the tip of his knife. His eyes

Wall of Silver

widen at a bright flash of light. He gasps and mutters, "My God! It's a piece of nearly pure silver." After searching the area and unable to find more, he builds a campfire. As he sits on his bedroll watching the thick smoke rising from the fire, he is startled when the smoke suddenly swirls and drifts off to the south.

Curious, he throws more green branches on the fire and watches. When the same thing happens, Jake takes a smoldering branch from the fire and waves it over a rock pile at the base of the cliff. When he detects a strong flow of air coming from underneath the pile of rocks, he feverishly begins to remove rocks from the pile until he exposes a stacked wall of rotting timbers. Almost certain that he has found a lost mine, he suddenly is filled with fear when he thinks about the last time he had found one.

He was a young, inexperienced field geologist at the time working for the Galena Mining Company. He recalled how he had been gathering rock samples in the high country when it happened. He had just set a string of charges along the base of a ridge. When he set off the dynamite, it exposed the entrance to a lateral mine. Expecting to find possible treasure, he threw all caution to the wind and it nearly cost him his life. When he entered the mine, he hurried through the main tunnel and entered the first drift that he came to. It was there that he came upon the skeletonized body of a lone miner lying face down with a bullet hole in the back of his head. It was evident that the miner had been taken by surprise, a rock chisel still in his outstretched hand. In a panic, Jake remembered that, leaving the mine, he turned the wrong direction in the main tunnel and ran right into the body of a second man who had been caught in the jaws of a large

The Discovery

bear trap that had been suspended from the ceiling. He could still hear his own screams as he struggled to free himself from the skeleton.

A later investigation of the incident revealed that the man caught in the trap was indeed a poacher and murderer. This conclusion was based on the fact that the gun found beneath the man's outstretched hand had one bullet missing from its chamber. A further report stated that numerous bags of silver were found in the rear of the mine waiting for shipment to the U. S. Mint.

After Jake removed the timbers from his newly found mine, he returned to the farm. Not telling his ailing grandfather of his discovery, Jake gathered up all his mining maps, spread them out on the kitchen table and searched for the lost mine. Unable to find any signs of it in the area, he figured that it had to predate the nearby Cliff Mine of 1841. When Jake returned to his campsite the next morning with all the necessary gear for going underground, he was still fearful. As he stood in front of the menacing-looking tunnel, he thought, " I wonder if it's trapped?"

When he thought of the desperate situation he and his grandfather were in, he muttered. "I've got to try it!" After crushing out his cigarette, he located a large round boulder and tossed it into the tunnel. As he listened to it roll down the slight slope and crash at the bottom, he thought, "Jesus, I hope I tripped any possible traps in the tunnel." Still apprehensive, he tied a heavy round fishing sinker to the end of a thick cord and lowered it down the tunnel. After it reached bottom, he pulled it back to the surface and measured its length. Next he uncoiled a heavier rope and measured it, allowing for tied knots some three feet apart. He tied one end of the rope around

Wall of Silver

This mine of 1841 is a relatively short distance from the "Wall of Silver Mine."
Photo credit: Michigan Technological University Archives and Copper Country Historical Collections.

The Discovery

the base of a nearby tree, weighted the other end of the rope and tossed it into the tunnel.

As insurance for not being trapped in total darkness should his carbide lamp fail, Jake strapped on a backpack filled with candles and matches. After lighting the carbide lamp on his hard hat, he put it on. Before slipping on a pair of leather gloves, he moved closer to the tunnel. A religious man, he said a silent prayer and backed into the unknown.

As he moved downward one knot at a time, he noticed that the tunnel was surprisingly dry. At the twentieth knot he looked upward, but the light at the surface was gone, indicating that the tunnel curved on its downward path. At the thirtieth knot, some ninety feet below the surface, Jake's foot brushed something metal that moved. Gripped with fear, Jake froze. Sweating profusely, he rolled over slowly on his back and looked between his parted legs. There in the beam of his lamp, he saw the closed jaws of a bear trap that was big enough to cut off the legs of an intruder. When he saw the shattered pieces of the boulder he had thrown down the tunnel, he breathed a sigh of relief and whispered, "Thank you God!" After brushing the trap aside, he realized that he was at the end of what appeared to be an escape tunnel. Cautiously rising to his feet, he looked around. As his light penetrated the total darkness, he saw that the front of the mine had collapsed, trapping the early miners underground. He also felt that someone was crushed by the cave-in because a shattered wheelbarrow was protruding from the rubble. As he scanned the fairly large mined-out area, he was startled by the reflection off of a pair of wire-rimmed glasses that were sitting on a crudely built table a short distance away. He asked himself, "Why

Wall of Silver

Near the old Cliff Mine.

Photo credit: Michigan Technological University Archives and Copper Country Historical Collections.

The Discovery

were they left behind?" He surmised that they were left as a memorial to the miner who was killed by the cave-in. As he moved cautiously through what appeared to be the main tunnel, he observed rock chisels driven into the rock on both sides of the tunnel at about ten-foot intervals, and hanging from them were strange-looking lanterns. He also noticed that the mine was relatively free of dampness because the heavy plank boards beneath his feet were intact. Some sixty feet into the main tunnel an opening to his right led him into what looked like a storage room. Supported by a number of rock pillars that had been left in place, it had been lighted by a number of lanterns that still hung from the walls.

Jake marveled at what he saw, it was a potpourri of lost history. Left neatly in place as if waiting for a later return of their owners, various mining tools lined a portion of one wall. Lined up on another wall were odd-looking wheelbarrows shaped much like a slice of pie, their sides tapered to a point where a wooden-spoked steel rim was fastened in place. They were in surprisingly good condition; a legible name on their sides read: " Hudson Bay Trading Company - At the Sault." After leaving the storage room, Jake moved further through the main tunnel until he reached a crosscut tunnel that was cut

Wheelbarrow similar to this was found in the mine. Sketch by Author.

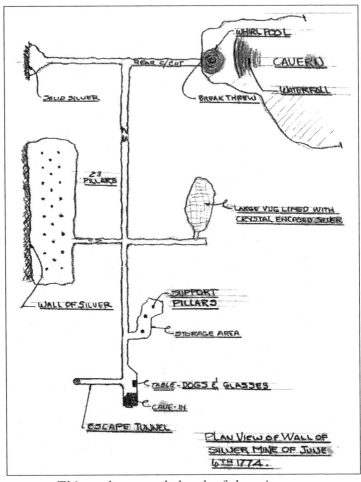

This underground sketch of the mine was produced by the author.

in a north/south direction. After he carefully followed the tunnel to the south for a short distance, it opened up into a large area where considerable mining had taken place, with numerous rock support pillars left in place. Jake noticed a large stope (previously mined area) that was filled with what looked like broken ore. When he

The Discovery

inspected it, and checked it with the tip of his knife, he was stunned when he found it to be rich silver ore. Overwhelmed by the wealth around him, he continued deeper into the mining area until he reached a wall of what looked like it had been chewed by giant rats. He was ecstatic when he found it to be a solid wall of silver. It appeared to be at least ninety feet long and vanished into the rock at both ends; it was impossible to tell how large the mass might be. As if stunned, Jake stared at the wall and thought of the nearby Cliff Mine, recalling that they had mined over two million ounces of silver from it in the past year. In thought, he muttered, "This has to be the mother lode that they've been looking for." It was evident that the early miners had difficulty trying to mine the pure silver because numerous empty kegs of black powder were stacked neatly against a nearby wall. In order to mine the silver, they had to use "moon chisels," shaped much like a new moon on one end and exceptionally sharp. A miner could peel off the relatively soft silver as easily as one could peel an orange. The wall had been mined so much this way that it gave off

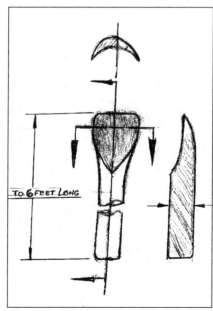

Steel moon chisel for peel-mining pure silver ore. Sketch by Author.

Wall of Silver

the appearance of a large piece of swiss cheese. As Jake studied the wall in its entire length, he noticed at one end some names had been carved into it. Although most were barely legible and difficult to read, one name stood out. It was "Sabin Stone," dated "June 6, 1774." Unable to connect the name with any part of early history, Jake looked around and thought of how his life would change. No longer would he have to worry about the cost of hiring someone to take care of his ailing grandfather.

He knew that it would be hard work hauling the silver to the surface but it would be worth it. Totally exhausted and in need of rest, Jake slipped off his backpack and removed some candles. After lighting a few, he puffed up his backpack for a pillow and lay down. With his head filled with thoughts about how his life would change, he closed his eyes and listened to the distant sound of rapidly moving water. Soon he was fast asleep.

Suddenly, he was ten years old. It was a beautiful Sunday morning, and the Central Mine was having its annual picnic at Lac Labelle. At the time there was a large dance pavilion built over the water. On shore with the other kids, he could hear a band playing and people singing. Then, all of a sudden, women started screaming, and men were shouting. Before anyone could make it to shore, the overloaded pavilion collapsed and sank in deep water. Before the shouting and screaming stopped, sixteen people had drown, including Jake's parents. Suddenly, he could see himself at his parents' funeral. He could never understand why his parents were not buried in the family plot. He never asked. Left with no other relatives to care for him, he went to live with his grandparents on their farm. He recalled that his grandparents treated him kindly but thought that they

The Discovery

were unhappy because they never smiled at each other, and they never slept in the same bedroom.

He also saw himself as a teenager. He remembered when he quit school at the age of fourteen, against his grandfather's wishes, and got a job working underground at the Galena Mine. He remembered how scared he was carrying dynamite packed in ice to the miners and blasters deep in the mine. He recalled how he roamed the high country as a teenager, searching for rare rocks and minerals, and how his collection eventually became recognized as being the best in the Upper Peninsula. While his collection was on display at a rock and mineral show in Houghton, Michigan, he recalled meeting the chief executive officer of Galena Mining and selling him one of his rare mineral specimens. From that meeting and sale, the man became his mentor. Jake's future soon changed at Galena Mining. No longer did he have to work underground; instead he was assigned to be a field geologist's helper working above ground. As a birthday present, Galena Mining awarded him a full scholarship to attend the Houghton College of Mining. Unfortunately, his grandmother never got to see him graduate because she died of a stroke six weeks before his graduation, and his grandfather was bedridden from an unknown illness. Faced with taking care of his grandfather, who was left nearly penniless from an earlier depression, he hired a live-in male nurse to care for him.

Awakened by an earth shock that rocked the entire ridge, Jake bolted upright and looked at his watch. He had been underground nearly three hours. Before he extinguished the candles, he picked out some silver specimens from the nearby stope and placed them in his backpack. Compelled to investigate the sound of

Wall of Silver

fast-moving water, he headed back to the main tunnel and turned to the west. Fearful that the rear crosscut tunnel might be trapped, he dropped to his hands and knees and crawled in. He was shocked to see that the early miners had broken through the end of the tunnel into what looked like a black void. Between the nearly deafening sound of roaring water and the strange feeling that he was being drawn into what looked like a bottomless pit, Jake thought of turning back but brushed his fear aside. Feeling it unsafe to crawl, he flopped on his stomach and wriggled his way toward the blackness. When he looked over the edge, he was shocked to see, not more than ten feet below him, the enormous eye of a large whirlpool that was spinning so fast it sucked the mist above it down its center. When Jake's light pierced the darkness beyond the whirlpool, he could see a large

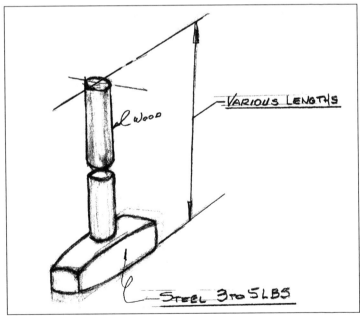

Typical hammer. Sketch by Author.

The Discovery

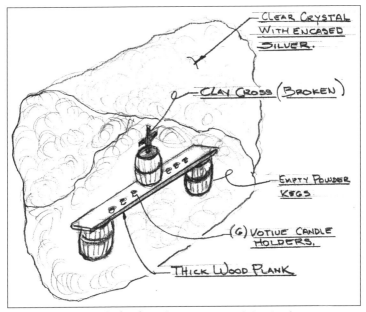

Make-shift altar in vug. Sketch by Author.

waterfall cascading into a churning body of water that formed the whirlpool. After Jake backed away from the break-through and got to his feet, he muttered. "This has to be the gateway to hell!" From the rear of the mine, Jake hurried to the north/south tunnel where he had seen the wall of silver and turned north. After scanning the walls of the tunnel for some distance, his light exposed an opening big enough for a large man to squeeze through. After checking it for traps and finding it safe, he entered it. When the beam penetrated the darkness, it exploded into what looked like a million stars. Awestruck by its beauty, Jake recognized what it was. Rarely seen in a miner's lifetime, it was known as a "vug" or crystal-lined cavity. He couldn't believe its size. Irregular in shape, it looked to be some twenty feet high at its lowest point and approximately forty feet wide, at its narrowest point.

Wall of Silver

When he walked off the length of it, he guessed it to be about sixty feet long. After he lighted a number of candles and placed them in various locations, the vug glowed with a heavenly sheen. To add to its beauty, not only was the vug lined entirely in clear, sparkling crystal, but it encased all types and sizes of gleaming pure silver as well. As Jake studied the vug and walked about, he noticed a makeshift altar at the far end of the geode. A closer examination of the alter showed that a number of wooden planks had been set on top of empty powder kegs. In the middle of the altar, and stuck in a keg filled with sand, only the vertical part of a cross made of miner's clay remained standing while the horizontal cross piece lay on the floor. Adding to the sacred setting, on each side of the cross were three candle holders, and in them the residue of votive candles. After taking a last look at the beauty around him, Jake returned to the surface.

History

1770–England was at war with France over the Northwest Territory of the United States and Canada. At stake was the lucrative fur trade. In an effort to control the free world, England suddenly found its treasury nearly depleted. When word reached General Gage, commander of all British Forces in North America, from an outpost in the Upper Great Lakes Region, that Indians were seen wearing trinkets of gold and silver, Gage sent word to England of the sightings. At the time when word reached England, it caused such an uproar that Parliament went into special session and a consortium representing the nobility was formed to finance the Alexander Expedition. At a lavish party thrown by the nobility, Sabin Stone, son of Lord and Lady Stone, was given a handcrafted leather-covered journal and carrying case and told to keep an accurate account of the expedition's travels and expenses for both the consortium and the Parliamentary Record.

Wall of Silver

In the spring of 1770, a sailing ship left England with Alexander Henry, Crown geologist Sabin Stone, and seven hard rock miners from Valley, Wales. After landing in Boston, the expedition traveled overland and canoed through rivers and lakes until it reached the British Settlement at Sault Ste Marie. During the winter of that year, plans were made to search for gold and silver. Because they feared traveling overland through hostile Chippewa Territory where no white man had been, a sailing sloop of some forty tons was built for them at Point Aux Pins near Sault Ste Marie.

In the summer of 1771, Henry, Stone and the seven miners set sail. With provisions for two years and no maps or charts to guide them, they followed the shoreline around the lake on the south shore to where a river (presently known as the Ontonagon River) emptied into the Big Lake (Superior). There, based on a rumor that gold could be found, they went ashore.

With a mining camp built, and their provisions secure, their search for gold and silver commenced. While the miners and Stone stayed at the mouth of the river to prospect, Alexander Henry returned to Sault Ste. Marie to spend the winter.

In the spring of 1772, a boatload of provisions was sent to the mining camp, Unfortunately, the miners were unable to find any gold or silver but instead found an abundance of nearly worthless copper. In June of that same year, the miners and Stone boarded their boat and returned to the Sault.

After the expedition failed, history records show that Henry left the Sault, journeyed south to Fort Mackinac, and eventually reached Detroit. As for the seven miners, they stayed on at the Sault to work as trappers for the

History

Hudson Bay Trading Company. With his knowledge of the precious metals he was seeking, Stone theorized that wherever copper could be found, gold and silver should be nearby. In the summer of 1772, after studying the ways and customs of the Chippewa Indians, Sabin Stone hired a half-breed, Jacques Quinte', to be his guide and interpreter.

On a warm summer day, on foot, carrying provisions and mining gear, Stone and Quinte' entered the Chippewa Territory. Within a few days of the Sault, as they broke camp one morning, they found themselves surrounded by natives brandishing spears. Half Chippewa himself, Quinte' explained to the band's leader that he and Stone were on a peaceful mission of exploring and that they would willingly respect the ways of the Chippewa, they were allowed to continue the journey.

Although gentle and courteous, Stone could strike fear into any man. Standing nearly seven feet tall, dressed in buckskin, a beaver skin hat, and a bearskin coat, and with his curly blonde hair and bearded face, Stone looked more like a mountain man than the son of aristocratic parents. Never before had the Chippewa seen such a giant of a man. Throughout the territory word soon spread of his presence. Among the Indians, Stone became known as "Walking Big Tree." In time, Stone became almost a God among the tribes. In spite of finding no gold or silver after a month into the journey, Stone was not discouraged. Aware that there was land to be discovered, they continued on in a westerly direction across the Upper Peninsula. Although travel was difficult at times because of the dense woods and rocky terrain, the two men met no real danger. At times, the journey offered the two men a quiet peace until one unforgettable morning. Because of the tragedy they witnessed this day, Stone felt it fitting to be the first entry in his journal.

The Journal

June 20, 1772

It was early morning, the woods were exceptionally quiet. Jacques Quinte' and I were panning a small stream for gold. Suddenly the silence was shattered by the blood-curdling screams of a woman some distance away. Startled by the desperate cries for help, we bolted to our feet and listened. When we were able to determine what direction the sounds were coming from, we grabbed our rifles and climbed to the top of a nearby ridge. From our hidden vantage point, as we scanned the landscape below, we saw two white men standing over a nude young Indian woman lying on her back in the meadow below, seemingly begging for mercy. As the woman struggled courageously, both Quinte' and I cringed when one of the men raised a cavalry sword over his head and brought it down hard across the woman's throat, severing her head from her body. As the angry man wiped the woman's splattered blood from his face, we could hear him cursing

Wall of Silver

as he kicked the severed head into the tall grass, and he laughed as the headless body thrashed about. Still not through with their grisly act, the two men began butchering the body. After cutting off the woman's limbs, breasts and other pieces of flesh, they placed them in a sack. When I asked Quinte' if he knew them, he told me that they were the Levec brothers whom he'd seen on occasion at the settlement in Sault Ste Marie.

I remember the rage that both Quinte' and I felt when he grumbled, "Lets kill the bastards!"

In silent anger, I looked down at the ghastly sight and fired a shot at the man with the sword but missed as he disappeared into the swamp. While I reloaded my long gun, Quinte' braced himself against a nearby tree and squeezed off a shot at the man carrying the sack. As the sound of Quinte's powerful rifle echoed across the meadow, I saw the trapper stagger and fall. Uncertain if the man Quinte' shot was dead, we cautiously moved into the field and found the lifeless body of a man with the back of his head missing. A short distance from the man's unwashed foul-smelling body, Quinte' found the sack that the man was carrying. When he picked it up and opened it, he cried out, "Oh my God!"

Quinte' convinced me, overwhelmed by the heinous act and uncertain what to do with the body parts, that they should be taken to the nearest Indian village; otherwise we might be blamed for the murder. As we cut across the field and headed for a village that was less than a mile away, our attention was drawn to a faint whimper coming from a nearby stand of trees. When I pushed aside the brush, we found another Indian woman tied to the base of a tree, stripped naked, badly beaten, and barely conscious. When she tried to speak to Quinte', he recognized her as being the eldest daughter of Chief Noka, the "Main Chief" of all the Chippewa Indians in the territory. She was too weak to walk and barely able to stand. I covered her with my shirt and placed her over my shoulder. With Quinte' leading the way carrying the bloodstained sack and the dead man's rifle, we soon reached the Indian village. We were met by a small band of Indians brandishing spears, already aware of our coming. Impatient with the menacing crowd, Quinte' shouted to their leader, "Take us to Chief Noka immediately; we found Princess Lilly injured."

The leader of the braves took both Quinte' and me to the lodge of the chief. In the center of a dimly lit room, the old man sat cross-legged on a thick bearskin rug. In keeping with his status, the chief wore a regal headdress of feathers and was dressed in buckskin and beads. When Princess Lilly heard her father's voice, she began to struggle so I put her down. When her father saw her battered face, he asked Quinte' , "What happened to her?"

When Quinte' told him of the violent attack that we witnessed, the chief asked to see the slaughtered woman's head so that he could identify her. I'll never forget that moment. When the old man reached into the bloodstained sack and pulled out the severed head by the hair, his eyes widened in horror. A religious man, he cried out, "Oh my God! It's my youngest daughter!"

After the chief regained his composure, he ordered all his braves to organize search parties and to bring Levec back alive. Before the sun had set, word of Levec's savagery was spread throughout the surrounding territory.

Wall of Silver

June 21, 1772

At daybreak, hundreds of braves, who had transformed their faces to look like birds of prey, gathered in the meadow where Levec had escaped into the cedar swamp.

June 24, 1772

Three days have passed since the search for the barbaric Frenchman began. Holed up in a beavers habitat deep in the swamp, Levec made his stand. After killing three braves with his rifle, he ran out of ammunition. Not wanting to be taken alive, he drew his sabre and fought with fury until he was subdued. Stripped naked and tied to a limb from a tree like a hunter's prize, Levec was bitten mercilessly by mosquitoes, deer flies and black flies. By the time his captors reached the village, Levec's body was a mass of swollen, bleeding flesh. Amid shouts for revenge, Levec was cut from the limb and dragged to the main lodge and forced to stand before Chief Noka. While two muscular braves held Levec tightly in place, the chief rose to his feet. Able to speak in Levec's native tongue, the chief glared into the eyes of the man who had murdered his beloved daughter and cursed him violently. When Levec spit in the old man's face, the chief flew into a rage and yelled, " When the moon is full, you bastard, you will die by the most tortuous means for the evil deeds you have committed."

In the center of a large ceremonial field not far from where Levec was being held prisoner, a shallow pit was dug and heaped with firewood, a short distance from the pit and six feet apart, two tall posts were set in place. Across the nearly eight-foot tall posts, upper and lower poles were added and tied in place.

The Journal
June 25, 1772

Throughout the day of the full moon, natives from the surrounding territory arrived at the village to witness the demise of the infamous Frenchman. By nightfall, a perimeter of fires glowed around " the pit of fire" and "the frame of death." When the beat of the drums stopped, all eyes focused on the Main Chief and his beautiful daughter, Princess Lilly. Dressed in elaborate ceremonial clothing, they were led through the crowd by two braves to a blanket inside the ring of fire. As drums beat softly, and before they sat down next to Quinte' and myself, the chief raised his hands to the full moon and said softly, "Let the sentence of death by torture begin."

After the shrill of voices from the restless natives subsided, and the beat of the drums stopped, all eyes turned in the direction of the lodge where Levec was held prisoner. Freshly bathed and stripped of all his clothing, with his hands tied behind his back, and a rope around his neck, Levec was pulled from the lodge and led to the frame of death. After a struggle took place, Levec was flipped upside down and his ankles tied spread eagle to the top crossbar. As Levec struggled unsuccessfully, his wrists were tied to the lower crossbar. Moments later, the Main Chief rose to his feet and moved slowly toward the man that had murdered his daughter. Filled with the need for revenge, the chief said loudly in Levec's native tongue, "Now evil Frenchman, it's your turn to die."

Before the old man sat down, he turned to the anxiously awaiting crowd and said for all to hear, "Let the revenge of our departed loved ones begin."

When the roar of the Indians subsided, and the beat of the drums began, the three widows of the slain braves stepped forward from beyond the ring of fire. Dressed in

Wall of Silver

ceremonial robes and carrying the sharpened hunting knives of their slain husbands at their sides, they moved slowly toward the pit of flames. When they reached the flaming pit, they handed the knives to three waiting braves who placed the knives in the fire. After they were heated white hot, they were given back to the three widows, who then headed for the frame of death. When Levec saw them advancing toward him with the glowing knifes, he thrashed about wildly and begged for mercy. While Levec was held in place by two husky braves, the infuriated widows applied the heated blades in an extremely systematic and devastating way, to every part of Levec's muscular sweating body. When the screams of intense pain and the smell of his burning flesh filled the night air, the blood-thirsty intense natives yelled, "More! Give him more!"

When Levec finally lost consciousness, cold water was thrown in his face to revive him. By the time their torture was through, most of Levec's quivering body was a mass of seared flesh, and he was on the verge of death.

After the three grieving widows left the frame of death and disappeared beyond the ring of fire, the disturbed crowd still chanted for more.

June 27, 1772

On this morning, as the village slept, a young man woke me and told me that Chief Noka wished to speak with me. Grateful that I was a part in saving his daughter's life, he offered me her hand in marriage. I was overwhelmed by his offer. I had fallen in love with her savage beauty the moment I set eyes on her.

The Journal

June 29, 1772

On this day Princess Lilly and I were married by a Jesuit priest. Following the elaborate ceremony, Chief Noka gave me a beautiful heavy belt of hammered silver. While in the priest's presence, I asked the Chief where the silver came from. I was told that it came from the River of Eagles.

"How far is that?" I asked.

The priest answered, "I just came from there, and it took me nearly forty-five days on foot."

"Can it be reached by a sailing ship?" I asked.

"Most definitely!" The priest replied.

I made a decision that day: we were going back to the settlement at the Sault.

July 10, 1772

My wife, Quinte' and I arrived safely at the Sault today. The first thing I did was to contact the British Agent at the Hudson Bay Trading Company. With a promise that the Crown would pay for the leasing of three sailing ships and all the necessary supplies I'd need for our journey to the River of Eagles, I gathered up sailing charts for that region and prepared to leave. With the help of the Hudson Bay Trading Company, I was able to locate the seven miners who had sailed with me on the Alexander Henry Expedition. When I showed them the silver belt that was given to me and told them where the silver came from, they were eager to join my expedition. For our safety on the Big Lake, I hired three able seamen to set our course.

July 19, 1772

With land always in sight, we reached the Keweenaw Peninsula shortly after noon this day. When we reached

Wall of Silver

the mouth of the Eagle River, we were met by friendly Ojibwa Indians who took us ashore in large river canoes.

July 20, 1772

The Indian settlement was rather large and its people friendly. After smoking a peace pipe with their leader, we traded axes, knives and beads for furs. When the trading was over, I had Quinte' ask if we could prospect for silver. After the tribe leader approved, he told us that silver had been discovered in a nearby river. As a friendly gesture, he ordered a number of braves to show us where it was found. Not far from the settlement, we entered the Eagle River, a shallow river with little current. We soon started to find silver nuggets the size of acorns. When the towering cliffs of the Greenstone Valley appeared, one of the natives pointed to the cliffs and told Quinte' "Go there!" Leading the way, the young brave ran to the base of the cliff and climbed a large rockpile. With his knife in his hand, he scratched the face of the cliff. When a bright surface caught my eyes, I knew immediately that it was silver.

When Quinte' asked the guides how the vein had been discovered, they told him that the day before they found it there had been a violent earth shock that caused parts of the Greenstone Cliffs to collapse. The next day when they were fishing in the stream, the bright morning sun reflected off of it. After a few days' rest at Eagle River, our party returned to the Sault.

July 29, 1772

Upon reaching the settlement at the Sault, we had a celebration and a meeting at the Cross Roads Tavern. At a table in a far corner of the tavern, while others looked on, I drew up the following document:

The Journal

This photo was taken near the Wall of Silver by the Author.

Wall of Silver

I, Sabin Stone, a geologist for the Crown and Ministry of Mines, London, England, on this day of July 29, 1772, in the Chippewa Territory of the Upper Great Lakes Region, with witnesses before me in an establishment known as the Cross Roads Tavern, at our Settlement in Sault Ste. Marie, announce and claim for the Crown of England, three quarters (3/4) of all silver that is taken from a mine, I shall name the "Silver Eagle Mine," which is located in a place called the Valley of the Greenstone Cliffs, a day's journey from the mouth of the River of Eagles.

By the power vested in me by the Crown of England, the other fourth of the silver mined shall be divided into twelve (12) equal shares for those who work said claim. Included for the Registry are those who exchange for their labors of the Crown. They are: Rufus Hall, Cyrus Hall, Anson Cheevers, Charles Lormis, John Langdon, Garth Hatfield, Josiah Sanders, Herman Cotton, Lewis Mayhur, William Bedford, Jacques Quinte' and myself, Sabin Stone.

After I signed the document to which my seal of authority was affixed, a duplicate was also signed by me and sent to England.

July 31, 1772

With my official document of intent, I reached an agreement with the Hudson Bay Trading Company at the Sault, which would provide the needed supplies to conduct silver mining and would also supply provisions to feed my party for two years. Because I feel the journey would be too dangerous to take my new bride along, I have made arrangements to have Lilly stay at her best friend's house, the Indian wife of Jean-Baptiste Caddotte at the Fort Repentigny Compound, a short distance from the Sault.

The Journal

August 3, 1772

Just after sunrise today we set sail for the Keweenaw. With good weather all the way, we expect to reach Eagle River within four days.

August 7, 1772

We arrived today at the River of Eagles shortly after noon. On shore, a large crowd showed up to greet us. In anticipation of our early return, a lodge large enough to accommodate all of us was built a short distance from the newly discovered silver. I was so overwhelmed by the Indian leader's friendship, I presented him with my rifle and my powder horn filled with enough gun powder and shot to last him through the coming winter.

August 12, 1772

We have been blasting and breaking rock for four days. Have established an opening in the face of the cliff large enough for me to walk upright. The Silver Eagle Mine went into production today with the removal of considerable silver ore.

October 3, 1772

Through the summer months enough ore was broken and hammered free of rock to fill our three boats to safe capacity. With the help of the friendly natives, it was hauled overland to the mouth of the river.

October 21, 1772

The boats have been successfully loaded with ore. They will leave for Pointe Aux Pins when the Big Lake is right to set sail. I prepared a map and letter to be given to my father, Lord Stone, informing him of the success and bright future of the Silver Eagle Mine. Six others and

Wall of Silver

myself will stay on through the winter to see if year-round mining is possible.

November 17, 1772
We have experienced our first snowfall. It is getting colder with each passing day. We are seeking to improve the camp for the winter months.

December 12, 1772
A severe storm hit us today. Working in the mine is impossible: drifting snow made the mine difficult to enter. As of today, without a break in the weather, I am shutting down the mining operation until spring. We all miss our families.

April 5, 1773
Somehow, we survived the winter without tragedy. We have endured a winter that none of us has ever witnessed. More snow fell in a matter of a few months than any of us had ever seen in our lifetime. Travel was nearly impossible. On days snow did not fall, all members of our party hunted for food. Luckily, we did not starve, as our supplies ran low more quickly than we anticipated. With the melting snow, our spirits have lifted greatly. As soon as possible, we will resume mining operations.

May 1, 1773
Snow has melted. Days are becoming warmer. We resumed mining operations today.

June 6, 1773
While cutting a north/south crosscut tunnel at the most rearward part of the mine, we encountered two geological phenomena. At the north end of the tunnel, we broke through into a large cavern that spilled fresh air

The Journal

into the mine. We are unable to see daylight in the cavern, only total darkness. A rapidly flowing stream could be heard in its depths. To our amazement, at the south end of the same tunnel, we encountered a solid wall of silver. It is so pure that our mining tools have been rendered nearly useless.

June 11, 1773

Learned today from Jacques Quinte', upon his return from the Sault, that I am now the father of a son.

August 4, 1773

A drift in the mine, cut to the south of the main tunnel, has intersected the same mass of silver that was discovered at the south end of the rear crosscut tunnel. Like the first mass found, it too, is so pure that it is virtually unminable.

August 6, 1773

Because of the incredible masses of silver that we have discovered, we decided to rename the mine, the "Wall of Silver Mine."

September 4, 1773

Tragedy has struck! Anson Cheevers and Cyrus Hall are dead. A massive cave-in has killed the two; the rest of us are trapped. The entrance to the mine has completely collapsed. We have a source of air coming from the cavern at the end of the rear crosscut tunnel. We are greatly saddened that the bodies of Cheevers and Hall cannot be retrieved.

September 5, 1773

The men are hungry. All are working feverishly digging an escape tunnel. Our only hope of surviving

Wall of Silver

lies in extending an escape tunnel near the front of the mine. If we can avoid intersecting the wall of silver, I believe our chances of breaking out onto suitable terrain are good.

September 6, 1773
We are steadily digging what we hope will be an escape tunnel. Our biggest fears are starvation and running out of candles and whale oil for our lamps. We have access to water from the cavern, but we need food.

September 7, 1773
Progress is slow. Exhaustion a problem. The men are restless from fear and lack of food. In hopes of reaching the surface sooner, we have started to angle the tunnel upward. Have encountered a large mass of copper in our path. We are digging around it and praying that the mass will not block our path. Candles and oil running low. I estimate only three days of light are left.

September 9, 1773
Our prayers were answered today! We have broken through to the surface near the base of the cliff. Although weak from lack of food, we have high spirits. The men are looking forward to their first meal in four days.

September 11, 1773
After a day's rest, William Bedford and I determined that the mine can still be operated by using the escape tunnel to haul the ore to the surface.

October 23, 1773
With our supplies running low and with winter soon upon us, we are all returning to the Sault, before the storms appear on the Big Lake.

The Journal

April 8, 1774

Supplies were charged to the Crown with the help of the trading company; our ships were loaded today. After considerable debate, we are taking our families with us.

April 9, 1774

Early this morning, our three ships set sail for the River of Eagles.

April 14, 1774

After seeking safe harbor three times because of the storms, we arrived safely this day at the mouth of the Eagle River without a mishap.

April 19, 1774

While the woman and children are staying at the lodge that was built for the men, all the men are being quartered at the mining camp.

April 20, 1774

We arrived at the mining camp early this morning and found it to be in relatively good shape.

May 2, 1774

There has been much rain in the last few days. The rain has quickened the melting of the snow around the opening to the tunnel we escaped from. We have inspected the tunnels of the mine and have found that they are intact. We have determined that by reworking some of the wheelbarrows into ore sleds and tying a rope to them, we can fill them with silver ore and pull them to the surface.

May 10, 1774

Mining operations have progressed steadily; with much labor, the ore is being pulled to the surface.

Wall of Silver

October 4, 1774

Our three ships were loaded with ore to capacity and left for Pointe Aux Pins. From there, I have made arrangements for the ore to be hauled overland and then loaded into river canoes bound for Montreal. With sufficient supplies available, and with our families providing extra hands for daily chores, we decided that we shall spend the winter.

November 14, 1774

Winter is fast approaching. Since early October, when our ships left for Pointe Aux Pins, we have been laboring in the mine.

December 2, 1774

We have received our first heavy snow. During the night, high winds have drifted over our paths and the entrance to the mine. Because of the snow and bitter cold, we will cease mining operations until spring. Since September we have mined and broken a good quantity of silver ore. We have stored the ore to near capacity in the drifts and stopes of the mine. In the morning, we will leave to join our families at the base camp.

February 10, 1775

An illness of unknown origin is spreading throughout our families, High fever has claimed the lives of Charles Lormis, his daughter Beth, little Tommy Towie, Lewis Mayhur, and his wife Katherine. It threatens to claim more.

March 2, 1775

The unknown illness has now taken nineteen members in our camp as of this date. We pray spring will bring us better health.

The Journal

March 29, 1775

The winter was cruel. Of the fifty-four members in our party who arrived here in the spring of 1774, twenty-one are dead. We are very sorrowful at the present time. We are awaiting the ships from Pointe Aux Pins that are due to arrive in early April.

April 8, 1775

The supply ships arrived in late afternoon today. Their appearance on the horizon of the Big Lake brought joy to the surviving members of our party.

April 10, 1775

Because of the many deaths in our mining operations party, we decided to close the mine until we return sometime in the future with additional miners. The thirty-three persons who survived the winter will set sail tomorrow morning.

April 11, 1775

We set sail from the mouth of the River of Eagles at daybreak. God willing, we hope to reach Sault Ste. Marie before the end of April.

April 23, 1775

Arrived at Sault Ste. Marie this day. The journey from the River of Eagles went well except for the additional death of young William Cotton, who succumbed to the mysterious illness that claimed the lives of so many others. I feel fortunate that my wife and young son Joshua survived. Resting from the long journey, I am waiting orders from the Crown.

Author's Note On Sabin Stone

In an effort to find out what happened to Sabin Stone after his last journal entry dated April 23,1775, I conducted an extensive search of history. With very little of history recorded at the time regarding the Upper Great Lakes Region, I contacted the "BIA," the Bureau of Indian Affairs.

There I learned of a man who might be able to fill in some of the missing links of early history in that region. His name was Chief Welsh, the ambassador of all the Indian nations. He was born in South Dakota in 1900, the grandson of famous Indian Chief Sitting Bull. I learned that I could contact him at the Indian Reservation in L'Anse, Michigan. I found him to be a very gracious man. We discussed early Indian history in the Upper Great Lakes Region. I learned that he had written a term paper while he attended Howard University entitled, "Indian Legends of the Upper Great Lakes Region."

Wall of Silver

When I discussed my writing a book on the Wall of Silver Mine, which I had visited, a glow of interest spread across his heavily wrinkled face. I asked him if he had ever heard of a man named Sabin Stone. He smiled and answered, "You must mean, 'Walking Big Tree'!" From that moment, I knew that I had found my source.

Chief Welsh turned out to be very knowledgeable on the subject. He talked of his childhood and when his grandfather told him the story of Walking Big Tree (Sabin Stone). He told me about the mutilation death of Chief Noka's daughter and the torture of a mad Frenchman who had killed her. He went on to tell me that Walking Big Tree, married the chief's eldest daughter and was given a belt of silver. When I asked him if he knew anything about what happened to Walking Big Tree, he said, "My grandfather told me that he must have drown when he was last seen fishing the St. Marys River, because his body was never found."

Unfortunately, after I left the Keweenaw Peninsula in 1974, I never saw Chief Welsh again.

Lee Stockard

Lee Stockard, Jake's grandfather, was born outside of Harrisburg, Pennsylvania, in 1841, the son of Dutch parents. During that period they owned the biggest dairy and cattle-breeding farm in the east. Educated in private schools and a graduate of West Point, he was commissioned a lieutenant in the army. When the Civil War broke out in 1861, he saw combat under General Grant. He was wounded in 1863 and recovered, and then sent to Washington for reassignment. At that time, the flow of native copper was most critical to the war effort. As a replacement for the procurement officer in the Copper Country, he was assigned to the War Department's Office in Houghton. It was there, while attending the annual Copper Baron's Ball that Lt. Stockard and socialite Sarah Prescott met and fell in love.

Before the Civil War ended, they were married in grand style. Lee was proud of his new bride and planned to take her to Pennsylvania to live. However, Sarah's domineering father thought otherwise. Pampered by her rich parents, Sarah was influenced to live in the Copper Country. In spite of strong objections, Lee Stockard consented to live in the harsh, isolated region. Familiar with the raising of cattle and dairy farming, Lee Stockard looked over the best farming land in Traprock Valley. With a grant from the President himself, Lee Stockard laid claim to the best four hundred acres in the valley, on which he planned to build his cattle and dairy farm. As a belated wedding gift, Howard Prescott, a former pharmacist who had become enormously wealthy on a modest mining venture, paid for all of the farm buildings that were built. Not to be outdone by his son's new father-in-law, Bart Stockard, Lee Stockard's father, shipped his son some of the best breeder cattle and dairy cows to start his own herd. With the farm run entirely by hired help, Lee Stockard and his beautiful wife traveled extensively and mingled with the rich in the area. For nearly three years, they traveled in the fast lane.

Eventually, Sarah wanted to settle down and have a child. Strangely, shortly after Sarah announced that she was pregnant, her husband auctioned off all of his cattle and laid off all of his hired help except those who serviced the house, and padlocked all of the farm buildings. Even more strange, when people offered to buy the farm, he refused to sell. When his son Andrew was born, instead of being a proud father, Lee Stockard seemed to ignore the boy. For years, he barely spoke to Andrew. Even when Andrew was old enough to work the farm, Lee Stockard refused to let him. When his son was old enough to get married, his father refused to give him the land he needed to build a house. Tired of his father's inexcusable bitterness, Andrew decided to homestead a

Lee Stockard

farm up in Central, a very isolated region, and to become a miner, an occupation that he feared. Even after Jake's parents drown at Lac Labelle, the old man couldn't shake his bitterness, for he refused to let his son and his wife be buried in the family plot.

The Confession

Eager to start removing silver ore from the mine, Jake had an ore sled built similar to those he had found. Familiar with the dangers of being trapped underground by either a cave-in or an intruder, Jake acquired some dynamite and primer cord to store in the mine. So that he wouldn't be solely dependent on his carbide lamp and candles, he purchased a number of kerosene lamps and a good supply of kerosene. To avoid having the mine entered without his knowledge, Jake removed all of the rotting timbers and replaced them with railroad ties. For added protection against intruders, he drove numbered nails into them so he could tell if they had been tampered with. To make it easier to haul ore from the stope to the ore sled at the front of the mine, he purchased a modern wheelbarrow and a bundle of potato sacks. To protect himself from possibly being seen, he decided to haul the ore from the mine under the cover of darkness. The first night he hauled ore to the surface, he counted eight bags

Wall of Silver

of about thirty pounds each. On his way back to the farm, he thought about where he could store it. Aware that he might need some heat, he decided that the milk storage building would be best because it was close to the blacksmith shop where there was a large fireplace. After he arrived at the farm and checked out the milk cooling house, he decided to dig a pit under the floor. He removed some of the flooring and began to dig.

With just the light from his kerosene lantern, he had dug a trench about three feet deep when his shovel struck something smooth and glanced off of it. Thinking that it was a rock, he jumped into the trench, brushed the dirt aside, and picked the object up. When he brushed it off, Jake got the shock of his life. He found himself looking into the eye sockets of a skull held in the palm of his hand.

When he turned it over, he found a hole in the base of the skull. After Jake carefully dug the dirt away from the skeletonized body he noticed that it wasn't clothed. He was unable to tell whether it was a man or woman until he removed a ring from the index finger of the left hand. He read the inscription inside the ring and knew right away that it was a man. Horrified, Jake leaped from the pit and ran to the house. After dismissing his grandfather's male nurse for the evening, Jake hurried into the old man's bedroom and called out softly, "Are you awake?"

When his grandfather answered gruffly, "What do you want?" Jake turned on a small lamp nearby and sat down on the edge of the bed.

When his grandfather opened his eyes, Jake said, "Gramps, I got a hell of a scare tonight, and I want to talk to you about it."

The Confession

"What happened?" the old man asked.

"I found the skeletonized body of a man under the floor of the milk cooling house. "Do you know anything about it?"

"That seems strange," he answered. "Did you report finding the body?"

It was obvious to Jake that his grandfather knew who the man was. When Jake showed him the ring, his eyes widened as he read the inscription. He started sobbing. He was eighty-six years old, and Jake feared he'd have a stroke if he pressed it any further.

A few days later, when he knew he was going to die, Jake's grandfather asked his grandson to get him his box of papers. From it he took out a print of his wife and himself on the day they were married. As he stared at the picture through tear-filled eyes, he said, "She was so pretty, and we were so happy at first."

After reading the inscription inside the ring again, he muttered, "The son of a bitch ruined our lives." Then he asked for his Bible. While holding the Bible, Lee Stockard said, "Your grandmother wanted to raise a family. When I couldn't give it to her, she started drinking and hanging around all the night spots such as the Michigan House in Calumet and the Douglas House in Houghton. Divorce back in those days was unheard of. Instead she left the farm and went to live with her parents. Without her in my life, I decided to auction off all my cattle and dairy stock and to visit my parents in Pennsylvania, hoping that Sarah would come to her senses and accept adopting a child."

Wall of Silver

Jake's Grandfather's Confession

"It was late when I stepped from the train. The weather was very hot and muggy. The moon was so bright I could read a newspaper in the night. I left my bags at the station and walked to the public stable and checked out my horse and buggy. I thought about stopping at the Michigan House for a drink, but I was afraid of seeing my wife. Instead, I picked up my bags at the station and headed for the farm.

It was past midnight when I got to the two-track that led to the farmhouse. The moon was still bright enough to see the farmhouse and the outbuildings in the distance. As I approached the house, I noticed a horse and carriage tied to the hitching post near the front porch. Not recognizing whom it belonged to, I went to the side of the house where the light was shining through the closed drapes of the bedroom window. As I stood by the open window, I heard my wife's voice and that of a man. There was laughter, giggling, and then silence.

Soon I heard heavy breathing and moaning, along with the sounds of the rhythmic squeaking of the bed. Enraged, something in my head seemed to explode. I went insane at the thought of another man sharing my bed with my wife.

Going to the barn, I unlocked the door to the black-smith shop and felt my way to the workbench. From a drawer, I took out my rusting Civil War service revolver. It hadn't been cleaned or fired in years. I flipped out the cylinder and ran the tips of my fingers over the bullets to see if it was loaded.

The boards on the front porch creaked as I reached for the unlocked door and slipped inside. Once inside, I paused until my eyes adjusted to the darkness. Like a cat,

The Confession

I moved past the kitchen towards the dim light that showed beneath my closed bedroom door.

Outside the door, I listened to the heavy breathing. Infuriated, I eased back the hammer of the gun. When the breathing reached a feverish pitch and my wife cried out in ecstacy, I barged into the dimly lit room. Before either of them knew what was happening, I fired twice. The man, in a partial upright position still on top of my wife, pitched forward when the slug from my first shot tore through the back of his head, out through his left eye, and into the heavy backboard of the bed. I fully intended to kill them both, but at the last instant, I changed my mind. Instead, I raised the barrel slightly and shot over Sarah's head into the wall. I can still see the wild look in her eyes as she struggled to free herself from her dead lover. Sitting up, with blood all over the front of her nude body, and the shattered eye of her lover lying between her breasts, she attempted to cry out but could not. Her body began to shake violently. Then she fainted.

Still in a rage, I pulled the nude body of her lover off of the bed and onto the floor. When I turned him over and looked at his face, I recognized him as Andrew Tippet. I saw that he had a ring on his finger, but there was no reason to taking it off. In a panic, I pulled his body over to the open window, pushed the drapes aside, and shoved him over the windowsill to the ground.

After washing the blood off of Sarah, I carried her unconscious body to another bedroom and placed her on a clean bed. When I returned to the scene of the shooting, I stripped the bed of its bloody sheets and pillows, gathered up Tippet's clothes and boots, tied them in a bundle and tossed them out the window. Next, I went outside to the shed and got a piece of cattle rope. It was

Wall of Silver

so bright I didn't need a lantern to see what I was doing. After moving my horse and buggy to the side of the house, I tied the rope around Tippet's wrists and pulled his body to the barn. After putting my horse in its stall, I took the bundle of bedding and clothes to the blacksmith shop, where I built a roaring fire in the hearth. I threw in the bundle and waited till they burned, after which I dragged Tippet's body to the cooling room and buried him beneath the floor.

When I left the barn and saw Tippet's horse and carriage, I realized that I had to get rid of them without arousing any suspicions. Left with no other choice, I decided to take them back to Calumet. Traveling on the outskirts of town, I walked the horse and carriage through the darkened back streets, tied them to a hitching rail in back of one of Tippet's bawdy houses, and started walking back to the farm. By the time I got there, it was near daybreak.

Sarah was still unconscious when I went into the house to check on her. After covering her with an extra blanket, I pulled up a chair close to the bed and waited. Thinking that I might face hanging for the murder of my wife's lover, I was prepared to hang. Strangely, two days later when she regained consciousness, Sarah couldn't move or speak. For days I took care of her as she lay in bed.

Over time, she regained her speech and the ability to walk. She rarely talked to me, so I have no idea if her memory was affected. After the murder, I knew that I could never sell the farm for fear that someone might discover Tippet's body. For that reason only, I remained in this harsh environment.

About eight months after the murder, your grandmother gave birth to your father. I knew he wasn't

The Confession

my son because past war injuries had made it impossible for me to have children. To make matters worse, your grandmother named your father Andrew after her dead lover. Although I was consumed by hatred, I know now that I was wrong in hating your father. To me, he was a bad memory haunting me from the past. As for your grandmother, I'm sure she loved your father with all her heart.

My grandfather's last words were, "Are you going to report the murder?"

I said, "No, Gramps, that would serve no purpose."

He smiled at me, and closed his eyes forever.

Against The Law

With seventeen barrels of high-grade silver ore stored in the barn, Jake sought out his favorite chair by the fireplace and deliberated on how to sell his silver.

From earlier days when he worked as a geologist's helper, he recalled how he found an uncharted mine that contained a fair amount of already mined silver ore, and how Salvatore Fattori illegally sold it for him. He had met Fattori at a rock and mineral show in Marquette when he sold him some rare rocks and minerals. A precious metals broker with offices in both Chicago and Houghton, Fattori was respected in the mining community. Confident that Fattori could help him, Jake decided to call him the next day.

"What have you got?" Fattori asked.

"A large amount of high grade silver ore to sell."

"How much?"

"Let's just say I've got an awful lot of it." Jake answered.

Wall of Silver

The two arranged to meet at noon the next day with Jake bringing samples.

Dressed in a business suit and carrying a large satchel, Jake entered the offices of Precious Metals Ltd. He noticed Fattori had aged considerably in the three years since he had last seen him. Dressed in an expensive dark suit and looking old enough to be Jake's father, Fattori appeared more like an underworld enforcer than he did a respected precious metals broker.

After the two men shook hands and talked briefly of former times, Fattori led Jake to a nearby conference table and said, "Let's see what you've got!"

Jake dumped the contents of his suitcase onto the table. Fattori took a small knife from his vest pocket, picked up a specimen, and scratched its surface. When a bright flash of silver pierced his eyes, he proclaimed it was a very high grade of silver. He asked Jake how much he had.

"Seventeen barrels," Jake answered.

Visibly surprised, Fattori asked, "How much do you expect to get for this?"

"You know better than I what it's worth, you tell me."

Without haggling, Fattori answered, "Thirty-five cents a troy ounce after processing."

The price was agreeable to Jake. The two men shook hands, Fattori repeated, "You say you've got seventeen barrels of this stuff. What did you do, find another lost mine?"

Jake answered, "That's precisely what I did."

The two sat down and Jake told Fattori what little he knew about the mine's history starting with this finding Sabin Stone's name and the date of June 6, 1774, carved into the mine wall. He continued, "I did some research on that period of time and found that the Alexander Henry

Against The Law

Terrain near the Wall of Silver. Photo by the Author.

Expedition left England in the early 1770s for the Upper Great Lakes Region to search for precious metals, but Sabin Stone's name was never mentioned."

Fattori brought the conversation back to the present time: "I noticed that your specimens are nearly free of rock and crystal. Did you clean them up?"

Jake said he found them that way and that there was enough broken ore in the mine to keep him busy hauling it out for years.

Astounded, Fattori asked, "Is there anything else unusual I should know?"

After a brief moment of thought, Jake asked, "Do you recall reading about the vug they found in a mine out in Cripple Creek, Colorado in 1890?"

"Do you mean the Cresson vug that yielded over $1,200,000 in gold?" Fattori queried.

Wall of Silver

"Yes, that's the one. There's a similar vug in this mine, but it's lined in silver rather than gold and it's out of this world."

Wanting clarification, Fattori said, "I've always been puzzled by the use of the word 'vug.' Can you describe one for me?"

Jake answered that "vug" cannot be found in the Merriam Webster Dictionary. In laymen's terms, the early miners called such a geological phenomenon a vug, but in reality it is a giant irregular shaped geode found in a pocket of solid rock."

Fattori interrupted, "By 'geode,' do you mean those round rocks that look like ostrich eggs?"

Jake said that, cut open, those "ostrich-egg"-shaped goedes are completely lined with crystal: "Picture yourself standing in the middle of a large irregular shaped cavity, lined in clear crystal much like a geode; then you'll have a pretty good idea what a vug looks like."

Satisfied with Jake's description, Fattori exclaimed, "Jesus Jake, that must look like something created in heaven."

"It looked so much that way that the early miners built an alter in it and conducted religious services there. I saw glass candle holders with votive candle residue still in them."

Familiar with the history of the early mines, Fattori asked if the mine was trapped.

Jake told the story of his experience entering the mine and encountering the bear trap.

Visibly moved, Fattori remarked, "My God, Jake, you could have died in that tunnel and possibly never been found."

Against The Law

Jake continued telling about his trip to the mine and discovering the cave-in. Fattori asked how the trapped miners were able to get a supply of air.

"Believe me, luck was on their side," Jake said, "because, after I followed the flow of air to the rearmost part of the mine, I got another surprise that scared the hell out of me." Jake went on to tell of his discovery of the abyss. Lighting a cigarette, he said, "When I worked my way to the edge of the tunnel and peered over, I was stunned. There, no more than ten feet below me, was a huge whirlpool spinning so fast that it sucked the mist above it down its large center. Because of the limited distance which my lamp could penetrated the darkness, I could barely see a large waterfall falling into a vast pool that formed the whirlpool."

Practically spellbound, Fattori asked, "Where do you think the water was coming from?"

"My guess is that it was coming from the melting snows in the high country. Although I did some research on the cavern and whirlpool, I couldn't find out much. My guess is that they were formed by one of the many volcanos that made up the Upper Peninsula millions of years ago."

"After the melting snow vanished, what happened to the whirlpool?" Fattori asked.

"I've seen it when it was just a small stream flowing down what I call a volcanic vent. When I got the nerve to look at the abyss when it was nearly dry, it was awesome. The sides of the hole were worn as smooth as glass and it was large enough for a big truck to be dropped into it without touching the wall."

Fattori wondered where all of the water went and Jake said he'd been told by fishermen that in the early spring

Wall of Silver

they've occasionally seen a water spout about about a mile off shore in Lake Superior, just west of the Greenstone Cliff Region.

Discussion of the water having been exhausted, "Something else that nearly blows my mind is how in the world did you manage to haul out so much ore?"

Jake explained by beginning: "Believe me, it wasn't easy! The first thing I had to do was set up some kind of a schedule because if some of the characters up here ever learned that I found the mine they might be willing to kill for it. I decided the only way to possibly prevent that from happening was to work the mine only at night and before the tracking snows appeared and after they melted in the spring."

Fattori asked how he protected himself from someone sealing him in the mine.

"I had one advantage of knowing if that happened." Jake said. He explained that he would immediately be able to feel a stoppage of the flow of air. In that case he hoped to blast himself out using the supply of dynamite he kept in the mine.

"How did you haul the ore to the surface?" Fattori asked.

"Much like the early miners did, with an ore sled. I built a more modern version of the ancient sleds left in the mine. I used wheels, and later casters, instead of the skids. At first I pulled the ore to the surface by hand but that was nearly unbearable for one man to do. After considerable thought, I managed to get my truck close enough to where I rigged up a rope-and-pulley system to pull the sled to the surface. I was hauling out an average of one half ton of ore a day under that system."

"Do you figure on hauling out more ore next season?" Fattori asked.

Against The Law

Truck similar to the one Jake Stockard used during his first year of operating the Wall of Silver Mine.

61

Wall of Silver

"Yes! If you think you can sell it."

"Oh! I can sell it alright. I just wanted to know so I can tell my processor what to expect," Fattori said.

Eager, Jake asked, "How soon can we expect to process this batch of ore?"

"I'll find out right now," Fattori replied as he reached for the phone. After a lengthy conversation, he turned to Jake: "They said they will be able to process it two weeks from today."

"What should I do in the meantime." Jake asked.

Fattori asked him what kind of truck he had and Jake told him a 1921 International one-ton speed truck. Fattori said it wasn't big enough and that he would have a truck and driver out to Jake's place the first of the next week. The ore would be taken to the loading dock in Dollar Bay. It would be shipped by steel barge, which would be tied to the dock waiting.

Fattori said he'd find out the exact time and give Jake a call. The two men shook hands and parted.

A week later, after dark, Jake received a phone call; it was Fattori.

"Are you ready to move out?" he asked.

"Yes. Steve's here to help me."

"Good! See you at the dock about midnight!"

Everything appeared to go well. Seventeen barrels of ore were off-loaded and later that night loaded aboard the waiting barge.

According to Jake Stockard those are his seventeen barrels of silver ore in the background.

Instant Wealth

Nearly a month passed after the ore was shipped. Then Jake received a call from Fattori. A jubilant Fattori exclaimed, "I've got a check for you; come to the office and pick it up."

Arriving at Fattori's office less than an hour later, Jake picked up his check and looked at it. He could hardly believe his eyes.

Concerned, Fattori asked, "Where are you going to cash that check?"

"I really don't know," Jake replied.

"So that you don't run into trouble hiding it from the local population, I suggest you come with me to Chicago and cash it there. At the same time I'll introduce you to my financial advisor who will launder it for you. You won't have to pay any taxes."

Jake agreed that it was a good idea and they arranged to go to Chicago together later in the week.

Wall of Silver

At the Chicago Bank that issued Jake's check, Jake met with Fattori's advisor. Due to the amount of money involved, Jake was advised to convert $35,000 of it into gold and to store it in a safety deposit box. Because of the rather volatile condition of the banking system at that time, he was also advised to keep the rest of his newly found wealth in ready cash.

From 1927 through 1933, Jake continued to prosper from the lost mine. Between his illegal sales of silver and from his investments in mining stocks, he became independently wealthy.

On March 5, 1933, when President Roosevelt ordered the closing of all banks, Jake made a trip to Chicago and on March 9, when the banks reopened, he removed all his gold coins from his safety deposit box and returned to the Copper Country.

Having no faith in the local banks, he had a special container built and hid his gold in the mine. Even though Jake drove fancy cars and escorted lovely ladies, most people in the region believed that he had made his money through selling bootleg liquor. Because of his large and fabulous rock and mineral collection, those who knew him well referred to him as the "Rockman."

In the summer of 1933, Jake started feeling uncomfortable in the high country. One night as he worked his claim, he felt that he was being watched. To protect himself, he varied his routes to the Cliff Region and would double-back on himself. On one occasion he got the shock of his life. Chills went down his spine when he caught sight of a man's disfigured face in the glow of his headlights as the man pulled his truck out onto the roadway. He was certain it was Nick Pinnelli, a hated union buster. Jake recalled meeting him at Galena

Instant Wealth

Mining. He was dressed like a gunslinger out of the Old West. Pinnelli didn't carry a gun, but he carried something far worse: he wore a custom-made belt filled with quarter size sticks of dynamite, and he always had a lit cigar in his mouth. Jake recalled that two union sympathizers were killed in a cave-in Pinnelli was rumored to have caused.

Feeling uneasy after seeing Pinnelli, Jake called off his plans for hauling ore and returned to the farm. Determined to find out what was taking place, Jake took meaningless trips throughout the Keweenaw Peninsula to see if someone would follow him. When he saw two cars bearing Illinois license plates, he called Fattori at his Chicago office and asked, "What in the hell is going on? I'm being followed constantly!"

Fattori answered, "There's a battle going on between two crime families that want to control the illegal silver market and right now you're their only source since most of the copper mines have shut down."

Perplexed, Jake asked, "Why didn't you warn me?"

Fattori said that he didn't have a chance because he'd been "practically a prisoner." He told Jake he thought there were plans to cut him out of the picture and he should not go near the mine: "You'll be safe as long as they don't find out the location."

Before Jake could say good-bye, the phone went dead.

On a stormy night about a week later, Jake was awakened by the sound of someone pounding on the door. When he answered it, he saw Fattori, white as a ghost.

He blurted out, "Before I left Chicago, I attended a meeting, and it was decided that the family wanted it all for themselves."

"What family?" Jake asked.

Wall of Silver

Fattori said it was the family in Chicago that was currently controlling the illegal silver market. They planned to follow Jake until he led them to the mine and then seal him in. As for Jake's argument that the mining company wouldn't tolerate any illegal takeover of their property, Fattori said, "You may think so, but those people have ways of making offers sometimes that can't be refused."

A visitor to the Copper Country in years past was treated to a startling illustration of the final play in this unusual game. Walking along the streets of a mining location like Greenland, Central, or Phoenix late at night, he could hear a weird tap-tap coming from the darkened homes of miners who should have been fast asleep. His guide explained calmly that the rhythmical beats were caused by otherwise honest miners breaking silver nuggets free of clinging rock. No one can say how much silver was extracted in those makeshift kitchen stamp mills but it is fairly certain that two of Chicago's wealthier families founded their fortunes on profits made from dealing in this extralegal silver.

From the book *Boom Copper* by Angus Murdock

"What were they using my silver for that suddenly led to this?" Jake asked.

Reaching into his coat pocket, Fattori took out a roll of halve dollars, handed them to Jake and said, "Look at these!"

After Jake opened the roll of coins and spread them out on the table, he asked, "What am I looking for?"

Instant Wealth

"Do they look alright to you?" Fattori prompted.

After studying the coins again, Jake remarked. "They sure look good to me!"

Fattori explained that the coins were struck with original dies that were scheduled to be disposed of by the United States Mint. He said the "Chicago family" had a set of dies for nearly every low mintage coin. The coins passed as mint strikes and sold in brilliant uncirculated condition for hundreds of dollars a copy.

"These people make fine silverware and other works of silver art and know the proper metal ingredients of every coin's makeup. Just imagine what they could do with your mine if they could somehow make a deal with the mining company that holds the mineral rights to that property." Fattori told Jake.

"Wow, what a racket!" Jake exclaimed. "Are they aware that you might be up here to warn me?"

Fattori admitted that he didn't know but said he'd been preparing for such a scenario by transferring his money and "squirreling it away in Canada," where his only relative, a brother, lived. As Fattori gathered up the coins and gave the roll of coins to Jake, he asked, "Did you ever manage to get your gold coins out of the bank in Chicago?"

"Yes, thanks to you," Jake responded. When Fattori said he hoped they were in a safe place, Jake told him they were hidden in the mine: "Maybe things won't work out for that Chicago crowd and I'll be able to retrieve them. I think, right now, my best bet would be to leave this place for a while and tour the country with my rock and mineral collection."

"Have you added anything special to your collection since I last saw it?"

Wall of Silver

"I sure have! Do you remember me telling you about the vug in the mine? Well, I took one of the largest broken chunks of crystal-encased silver from it that the world will ever see."

"Can I see it?" Fattori asked eagerly.

"Sure! You're a collector; you'll appreciate seeing it." Jake left the room and returned with a wrapped object about the size of a bowling ball. Under the overhead lamp above the kitchen table he removed the tin foil. When Fattori saw its crystal-encased beauty, he gasped and said, "My God Jake! This specimen is going to be a sensation every place you put it on display. What are you going to tell the press when they ask you where you found it?"

Jake said he felt he had no choice but to tell them that it came from a vug in a lost silver mine: "Maybe it will cause enough attention to hopefully help save the mine from destruction."

Fattori guessed what he was thinking: "You mean like have the government declare the mine a national historic site."

"But first I've got to get my gold out along with a ledger that contains weights of all the silver ore I hauled to the surface."

Surprised by Jake's shocking revelation, Fattori warned, "I hope you know, Jake, if that ledger falls into the wrong hands, we both could spend a lot of time in a federal prison."

"I know, it was foolish of me not to destroy them after the silver was sold."

Glancing at his watch, Fattori said, "I've gotta get moving."

Instant Wealth

As the two men embraced with tears in their eyes, Jake said, "Have a good life, and thanks for everything you've done for me."

The two men never saw or heard from each other again.

The Treasury Department

With a supply of the ore he had found in the vug, Jake toured the rock and mineral shows throughout the country. At all of them, with his "Sabin Gem' as the centerpiece, he became famous. Unaware that Fattori had contacted the Treasury Department and alerted them of the counterfeiting of coins that was taking place in Chicago, Jake continued to sell silver specimens from the mine to the demanding public. At the New York Rock and Mineral Show, Jake unknowingly sold silver specimens to two undercover treasury agents. Faced with a large fine and the possibility of many years in a federal prison, Jake hired a lawyer and filed a claim that, even though silver is a monetary metal, it did not apply to him in his case because he was selling his specimens as collector's items. For years the case traversed the judicial system until a ruling was handed down by a higher court.

Wall of Silver

On April 16, 1940, before a packed courtroom, the following ruling was read:

"All charges against Jacob Stockard have been dropped by the Federal Government because it has been ruled that Mr. Stockard cannot be charged with the sale of a monetary metal in the form of a specimen because it has been ruled that they are collectible, much like rare coins."

A foot note was also read: "After an exhaustive search of the region failed to locate the source of Mr. Stockard's obtained silver ore, it has been concluded that he must have found an uncharted mine."

When World War II broke out, Jake enlisted in the Corps of Engineers and spent most of his military career building and repairing airfields in the Pacific.

Historical Search

When the war ended, Jake returned to the Keweenaw Peninsula (sometimes called "Copper Country") and made his first attempt to recover his cache of gold and the ledger that could send him to prison. To avoid meeting anyone who might recognize him, he wore a beard and dressed much like a homeless person.

Renting an old car, he set out for the Greenstone Cliff Region. He was surprised that it no longer seemed to be as remote and wild as it once was; he saw numerous loggers and drilling crews in the area. Even at night, as he watched from the window of his rented cabin, he observed the mining company security patrols making their rounds. Realizing that the time was not right for his return to the mine, he made plans for leaving the Copper Country. Before he left the area, he rented the farm to his best friend Vern Parker and his wife Freda and put his finances in order.

Wall of Silver

Within the week, he arrived at Heathrow Airport in England. There he hailed a cab and headed for London, where he visited the British Library. Referred to the Public Records Department, he met a lovely young lady, twenty years his junior, and fell in love. After he introduced himself and explained what he was looking for, Katherine Allingham left the room. She returned within minutes with a file on the "Alexander Henry Expedition." As they searched through the file together, Katherine selected a document. After reading it, she passed it to Jake and said, "I believe this is what you're looking for."

It was the log and manifest of the HMS Monarch, dated May 16, 1770. It read: "On this day, we left the safe port of Liverpool for our Boston destination." Besides the lengthy list of cargo, the manifest revealed the names of its passengers. Among those on board when the voyage began were Alexander Henry, the expedition's leader; Sabin Stone, a geologist for the Crown; and seven hard rock miners from Valley, Wales. The names of the miners were:

Herman Cotton

William Bedford

Anson Cheevers

Cyrus Hall

Garth Hatfield

Joshua Sanders

Lewis Mayhur

After Jake got copies of the papers he needed, Katherine asked, "Are you going back to the states right away?"

Historical Search

"No," Jake said. "The first thing I'm going to do is celebrate this occasion. Would you care to join me for dinner, and a night of dancing?"

"I'd be delighted!" Katherine responded.

For nearly a year Jake stayed in England and his beautiful Katherine rarely left his side. After Jake gave her an engagement ring, he asked her if she would like to return to the United States with him while he continued his research. However, Katherine was reluctant to leave her very sick mother and they decided Jake should return alone. He boarded a flight to New York with connections to Sault Ste. Marie and began his search for the missing pieces of history.

He rented a car at the Sault and visited the Chippewa County Court House. Introducing himself as a historian, Jake explained to the records clerk what he needed and gave her a list of the men on the ship's manifest. The Clerk returned from the records vault with a smile on her face and said, "Were in luck. From the tax rolls, there is a man named Richard Stone who lives on a large Centennial farm about twenty miles south of here."

The next day as Jake turned his rented car into the driveway leading to the Stone farm, he saw a historical marker on the front lawn that read: "Homesteaded in 1802 by Joshua Stone."

A rugged, suntanned man, who looked to be in his mid-forties, met Jake as he left his car and walked toward the well-kept farmhouse. The smiling man, followed by his dog, asked what he could do for Jake.

"I'm a historian, and I think your family is a missing link of unwritten history. May I discuss your family ancestry with you regarding a man named Sabin Stone?"

Wall of Silver

"Of course, I'm Richard Stone and Sabin Stone was my great-grandfather," he offered.

Elated, Jake smiled and said, "I'm willing to pay for any information you might have."

Stone nodded his approval. As he led the way to the house, he said, "If it's history you're interested in, you've come to the right place, let's go into the house."

Inside, Stone immediately gave Jake a brief conversational tour of his family tree and then left the dining room. He returned with what looked like a manuscript box and set it on the dining room table. Exuding pride, he opened the box and placed its contents in front of Jake. When Jake opened one of the doeskin-bound holders, his eyes widened in delight. As he read the handwriting on the first page, he saw it appeared to be an original journal. As he continued to hunt through the aging treasure, he struck pay dirt when he found the signature of Sabin Stone, with the seal of the Crown of England affixed to the document. He knew that he had found the information he sought.

Jake stayed on at the Sault long enough for Stone to run him two copies of the historical documents. After paying Stone a substantial finder's fee, Jake left the States and returned to England.

When Katherine reviewed the documents that Jake had brought back from the Sault, they both concluded that Sabin Stone did attempt to contact General Gage and his father, but somewhere in that vast and dangerous wilderness, the courier never reached his destination. Had he done so, England may have been able to continue its domination over America and possibly the United States might never had been born.

Historical Search

A few months later, Katherine and Jake were married in an elaborate ceremony at a cathedral outside the town of Attlebridge, England. Jake was sixty-two years old and Katherine was forty two. For ten years they toured the world and enjoyed life to the fullest. Then Katherine died suddenly of heart disease. Brokenhearted, Jake returned to the place of his birth.

The Rockman

The winter of 1970 was severe in Michigan's Keweenaw Peninsula. With the coming of spring, high banks of snow still lined the shoulders of U.S. 41.

For Barb and Dick Kellogg, the owners of Sportsman's Bar, the winter was even more severe. With the closing of the copper mines and the absence of miners and above-ground workers, their once bustling business was now in a state of bankruptcy. Preparing for the coming of spring and, hopefully, tourists, Dick was building a display case to house his many specimens of copper that came with the purchase of the business.

While Dick was using his power saw, a pickup truck pulled into the parking lot and stopped. When an imposing-looking man got out and headed for the front door, Dick shut off the saw and waited silently as the man stepped inside. He was an older man with a deep tan, silver gray hair and a well-groomed beard. Well over six feet tall, he had to duck to enter the bar. He was ruggedly

Wall of Silver

This is the tavern in the Copper Country where the sales of silver specimens from the Wall of Silver mine took place.

The Rockman

handsome with a powerful build and deep wrinkles that lined the chiseled features of his face. He looked intimidating in his lumberjack-style clothes: a vest over a plaid flannel shirt and heavy leather boots. Instead of approaching the bar, the stranger moved slowly along the outer wall of the tavern as if he were looking for something. When he reached the far end of the room where a near-record speckled trout was mounted under glass, he paused. A smile spread across the man's face as he read the plaque beneath the fish.

Continuing on with his methodical inspection of the walls, he now focused his attention on the display case of rocks and minerals. After studying the contents for a few moments, he turned and moved toward the bar. When he saw that he was being watched, he reached out his hand and said, "Hi! I'm Jake Stockard!"

Dick grasped the outstretched hand and said, "I'm Dick Kellogg. I own the tavern. I bought the place three years ago."

Jake nodded his approval and, looking at the wood carving above the bar, he said, "I've always liked this place. I was here the day that it opened." After ordering drinks for the both of them, Jake asked, "Are you a collector of rocks and minerals?"

Dick said he wasn't but that they had come with the business. Fascinated, Jake asked to take a closer look at some of them, particularly "two pieces of crystal copper."

Surprised that Jake knew what they were, Dick asked, "Are you a collector?"

Jake said that indeed he had been a collector. After a closer look at the pieces, he said, "These are mighty fine pieces of native copper. They should increase in value now that the mines are closed because they are the last of

Wall of Silver

those that came from underground. If you need money," Jake added, "I don't think you'd have any trouble getting a good price for them from the tourists."

Never having seen Jake before, Dick asked, "Do you live around here?"

Jake answered, "I was born in these parts, but I've been in England for the last ten years. I just got back three days ago and plan to stay long enough to sell my grandfather's farm in Traprock Valley."

Familiar with the farm because he fished the river behind it, Dick said, "I thought Vern Parker owned that farm."

"I've been renting it to Vernon and his wife for nearly ten years," Jake said. "In fact, they have an option to buy it from me."

Dick remarked, "You know, the Trap Rock River that runs behind your place has to be the best trout fishing in the state."

"You bet it is!" Jake agreed and proudly pointed to the record speckled trout on the wall. "That's where I caught it." After ordering another round of drinks and sharing a pizza, Jake glanced at his watch and said, "I've got to be moving on. I just stopped in for a drink and a look at the old place."

"Sure glad you did. It's been a pleasure meeting you," Dick said as the two men shook hands.

A short time later when a beer truck pulled up out front and, when the driver came in with a case of beer in each hand, Dick asked, "Say, Paul, have you ever heard of a man by the name of Jake Stockard?"

Paul set the two cases of beer down and answered, "Who hasn't! Why do you ask?"

The Rockman

"I met him a couple of hours ago, and he told me he just got back from England."

The beer truck driver looked surprised and said, "So that's where he's been all these years. When he suddenly disappeared, everyone thought that he was dead."

"Why do you say that?" Dick prompted.

Paul told Dick what he knew about "the Rockman." "It was rumored that he had found a lost silver mine in the 1920s that made him independently wealthy, and that he possibly got into some trouble with the parties he was illegally selling the silver to. He was also a graduate geologist and owned one of the finest rock and mineral collections in the Upper Peninsula."

After Paul left, Dick spent the rest of the day in the emptiness of the tavern. When he shut down for the night and counted the day's receipts, there was barely enough to cover the cost of the lights. Extremely depressed as he drove three miles south to his home, he muttered, "If I'm going to keep the bar open, I'll have to go to the bank in the morning to see if I can get a loan."

It was noon when Dick left the main branch of the Merchant and Miners Bank in Calumet, Michigan. Not too surprised that he was refused a loan. But he was also told that he faced foreclosure on the tavern in ninety days.

He headed north to Sportsman's Bar. When he pulled into the parking lot to open for business, Dick reminisced how it once was. Customers no longer waited for him to open, unlike the days when the mines were running. It had been nearly three years since he had seen the large parking lot filled with cars. Now, except for his Jeep, the parking lot was empty. But, in spite of the fact that his

Wall of Silver

life-savings were nearly depleted, Dick was not ready to give up his business. He entered the bar.

Jake Stockard's comments regarding the value of his many copper specimens encouraged him. Aware that he had to come up with some kind of attraction to lure tourists into the tavern, Dick removed the rock and mineral collection from the showcase and stored them in the back room.

Returning from the storage room and stepping behind the bar, he heard a car door slam. Moments later Jake entered the tavern. In a happy mood, he called out, "Hey Dick! How are things going?"

"Hi, Jake. Slow as usual," Dick answered.

"Jesus, that's too bad! How about joining me in a couple of beers?"

With a bottle of beer in his hand, Jake ambled over to the empty showcase. When he returned to the bar and sat down, he asked, "Have you decided to sell your copper specimens?"

"Yeah! Business hasn't been good at all lately, so I thought I'd put some on display before the tourists start showing up in this neck of the woods."

Jake agreed with Dick's plan; then Dick changed the subject: "Whatever made you decide to live in England?"

Surprised by Dick's sudden interest, Jake replied, "It was purely by accident that I did. Back in the 1930s when I was a geologist, I planned to write a book about an uncharted mine that I found up here. I went to England to research some mining equipment I found in the mine. To make a long story short," he added, "I met a lovely lady, fell in love and got married. Unfortunately, now it's all history."

The Rockman

When Jake turned his head to look out the front window, Dick sensed that some tragedy must have happened in England to bring him back to the Copper Country. Jake looked back and ordered another drink. Dick could see that his eyes were moist with tears. Feeling bad and ill at ease, Dick quietly said, "Jesus, Jake, I sure didn't mean to upset you."

"Hey, forget it; you have nothing to apologize for," Jake insisted, giving no hint of what had upset him. After a few moments of silence, Jake asked about Dick's family and how they came to live in the Copper Country.

Dick said enthusiastically that he was married to a "lovely lady named Barbara" and they had two sons: Mark, seventeen, and Kurt, twelve.

Dick began to explain what brought him north, "At one time I was considered by the powers-that-be at General Motors to be a boy wonder. In 1939, at the age of thirteen, I was shaking hands with such men as Harlow Curtis, Harley Earl and Charles Wilson on the fourteenth floor of the General Motors Building. Unknown to me at the time was that my highly respected inventor and engineer father had taken some of my scale clay models of cars of the future to Harley Earl, then the head of G.M.'s styling. Who would ever think that thirty years later someone would be destroying my promising career at General Motors."

Dick said he blamed John DeLorean for conspiring against him. "All the men who sat in judgement of me worked for DeLorean," Dick said.

"Are you going to sue him?" asked Jake.

Dick said, no, but that instead he planned to write a book about the experience, titled "Lucky To Be Alive."

Wall of Silver

He continued, "When I lost my good paying position I could no longer afford to send my autistic son to private schools. After checking with the State Department of Mental Health, we found out there was a state-funded program in the Intermediate School District of the Copper Country that might fit my son's needs. After we came up here and checked it out, we decided that it was the only thing we could do. Before we sold everything of value that we owned, I made numerous trips up here to find employment or a business that would support my family. After finding nothing that showed any kind of promise except this place, I purchased the bar."

"Were the mines still operating then?" Jake asked.

Dick said they were but the miners were threatening to strike for better wages. "As luck would have it," he said, "Calumet Hecla decided to sell out to Universal Oil Products rather than settle the strike, and the mines were shut down."

Jake shook his head over Dick's bad fortune and said, "Jesus, Dick! I can understand how you got into this situation through no fault of your own." Feeling sorry for Dick, he asked, "I'm going trout fishing tomorrow, would you like to go with me?"

Dick answered in the affirmative, saying that Barb could open the bar for him.

After a successful morning of fishing the Trap Rock River behind Jake's farm, the two men were sitting on a log when Jake remarked, "I think I have something for your place that will attract tourists. It's the most beautiful silver specimen you'll ever see."

Excited, Dick asked, "When can I see it?"

The Rockman

"Right now it's in storage in Iron Mountain. I'll go there tomorrow and have it back here by Wednesday, and at the tavern by noon."

When his new friend arrived at the tavern as planned, Dick held the door open for Jake, who was carrying a locked Army foot locker.

"Where do you want me to set this?" he asked. "It's kind of heavy?"

Dick pointed to the top of the bar and Jake ordered him to close and lock the doors.

Dick asked why, and Jake answered, "Because you don't want to show any of this stuff to the public until you're ready."

After the room was secure, Jake turned on the light over the pool table as Dick watched. He opened the locked footlocker, reached inside and took out an object about the size of a bowling ball wrapped in tin foil and set it in the middle of the pool table. Without saying a word, he began to peel back the foil.

When the last of the foil was removed, Dick asked, "What is it?" It's beautiful."

Jake explained that it was probably the largest specimen of crystal-encased silver in the world. When Dick asked if he was afraid someone might steal it, he said, "Not really because everyone knows that it belongs to me. There isn't a museum curator in the country who wouldn't recognize it as mine."

Astonished, Dick asked where he got it.

"I found it in a silver mine many years ago," Jake replied.

"What's something like this worth?" Dick asked.

"I really haven't any idea," Jake answered.

"Is this what you're planning on loaning me for the center section of the display case?"

Wall of Silver

"That's right!" Jake beamed.

Feeling obligated, Dick asked if there was something he could do for Jake to repay the favor.

"I do have something you might be interested in," Jake answered as he reached into the footlocker. He took out another canvas bag and poured its contents onto the table.

Staring down at thirty pieces of rocklike objects, Dick didn't recognize them as silver specimens that had oxidized with the passing time.

"At one time, they were as bright as newly minted coins," Jake said. "I want you to sell them in the tavern and we'll split fifty/fifty."

"What are they worth?" Dick asked.

"Let's weigh one of them and find out," Jake suggested as he took a precious metals scale out of the footlocker and set it in front of Dick.

"How do we price them?" Dick asked as he placed a specimen on the scale.

Jake lit a cigarette and answered, "We sell them for fifteen times the quoted price of silver per troy ounce. It was a dollar an ounce yesterday."

After Dick finished weighing the specimen, Jake asked, "How much does it weigh?"

"Nine ounces on the button."

After figuring the price out in his head, Jake said, "That's worth $135."

"You've got to be kidding!" Dick exclaimed.

Jake assured him he wasn't and asked Dick if they could make a deal.

"You bet we can!" Dick agreed as the two men shook hands. "How much of this silver do you have?"

Dick thought it strange that Jake answered, "I don't know. I'll have to check and see if it's still there."

The Rockman

Realizing that Jake was in a hurry to leave, Dick asked, "How do we clean this stuff?"

"Dip them in nitric acid and a like amount of water," Jake explained. "Just remember, wear a mask and have lots of ventilation because one good whiff of that nitric acid can kill you!" After Jake left, Dick packed everything into the footlocker and put it in the storage room.

Crystal-Encased Silver

Nearly a week had passed since Jake traveled north on U.S. 41. Just north of the ranger station, his eyes caught sight of a billboard which read: "Sportsman's Bar - Home of the World's Largest Piece of Crystal-Encased Silver."

It was obvious that the new sign had caught the attention of many people, for, as Jake pulled into the parking lot, he found it difficult to find a parking space. As he left his pickup truck and headed for the tavern, he noticed a freshly painted sign in the window saying: "Silver Specimens for Sale."

On the first day that the collection was displayed, men and women were lined up outside the tavern waiting for Dick to open. From the first day that the silver was on display, Dick and his wife sensed that there was going to be trouble over where the silver came from. For those who didn't recognize Jake's famous specimen, Dick explained that it had been loaned to him by Jake

Wall of Silver

Stockard. As the day wore on, very few people left the tavern. Caught up in the excitement of seeing ten gleaming pieces of silver sold throughout the day, the boisterous hard-drinking crowd chose to remain to see if other specimens would be added to replace those already sold. In a far corner near the display case, four older men watched intently as they played cards and drank beer. A rugged bunch, Dick sensed they were trouble.

When Jake entered the tavern, Dick noticed that they watched his every move. In spite of the many years Jake had spent away from the area, most of the older people recognized him. To those he'd helped in time of need during the Great Depression, he was their Robin Hood because it was rumored that he obtained his mysterious wealth from what belonged to the rich and gave a great deal of it to the poor. To the local populace who had seen or heard of his fabulous rock and mineral collection, he was their legendary "Rockman."

As Jake stood by the door looking for Dick through the smoke-filled tavern, an older ex-miner stood up, raised his glass and shouted, "Welcome home, Jake!"

When most of the people joined in, Jake tipped his hat and called out, "Thank you! The next round of drinks is on me!" After the roar of the crowd died down, he walked directly to the display case, gazed down at his superb specimen of silver and muttered, "You still have your magic!" Sensing hostile eyes upon him, Jake stood motionless while he scanned the display case for the thirty pieces of silver he had given Dick to sell. Able to see only four of the smaller specimens remaining, he muttered happily, "Well, I'll be damned! He must have already sold the rest of them."

Crystal-Encased Silver

Aware that he was being watched closely for some reason other than being the "Rockman," Jake moved to the end of the display case where he could get a less conspicuous look at the men who were watching him. He gazed at the tough-looking bunch from the corner of his eye. He imagined erasing some forty years from their haggard, wrinkled faces, but even then he couldn't recall who they were. Considering that they were poorly dressed, and the way one of them coughed and fought for air, he assumed that they were all ex-miners.

It was only when one of them turned his head to talk with another that Jake recognized who he was. Jake cringed when he recalled the nights that Nick Pinnelli tracked him through the woods with a gun, hoping to find out where he had gotten the mysterious silver. Choosing to ignore him, Jake left the display case and headed for the bar. When he paid for the drinks he had bought for the house, he asked, "Is Dick around?"

"Yes, he is, Jake," the barmaid answered. "He told me he'd like to speak with you in the stockroom."

In the stockroom, after the two men shook hands, Jake asked, "How is it going?"

"It's hard to believe it's selling so well. I've got only four specimens left," Dick said.

Jake was curious who most of the customers were and what Dick told them his source was. Dick said mostly faculty from the Mining College and local businessmen were buying the specimens and he told those who asked that he found it near the base of the cliffs with his metal detector.

Jake asked, "Has anyone complained about how much your charging?"

Wall of Silver

Dick shook his head and said, "Not one! In fact I got the impression that they were willing to pay more."

Jake asked if Dick would be interested in selling more silver if he could get his hands on some.

Dick eagerly answered in the affirmative but expressed his hope that it wouldn't cause Jake any trouble.

"It might," Jake admitted, "but I'll worry about that when the time comes."

Shortly after Dick returned to the bar, a well dressed elderly man approached him and asked if all of the silver was for sale.

"Yes it is, would you like a closer look at it?" Dick said and handed him a jeweler's glass.

"How do you determine the price?" the potential buyer asked.

"I weigh them and charge $15 an ounce," Dick answered.

The silver was weighed and the price determined to be $150. After the man gave Dick traveler's checks in that amount, he left the tavern with his purchase.

Pinnelli turned to the man next to him and growled, "I wonder what the son of a bitch is going to do now that he's sold all the silver?"

The scroungy character next to him replied, "I don't know, but if any more of it shows up in that display case, I'm sure as hell am going to try to find out where it's coming from."

"Me too," Pinnelli growled as he gathered up the empty beer bottles from the table and headed for the bar.

Startled by the sound of beer bottles being set down hard on the surface of the bar, Dick turned around just as Pinnelli barked out, "Gimme four more Bosch!"

A chill went down Dick's spine as one piercing blue eye glared at him while the other lifeless orb reflected the

Crystal-Encased Silver

light off the back of the bar in it's glass pupil. Pinnelli was a mean-looking man, even without the deep scars that covered the right side of his face. Dick sensed Pinnelli was trouble when he sarcastically remarked, "I've lived around here all my life and ain't never seen silver like that, except when I worked underground in the Iroquois Mine."

"That may be true in your case," Dick snapped back, "but just maybe you've been looking in the wrong places." Angry, Pinnelli tossed the exact change on the bar, picked up his four beers, and headed for his table.

As the night wore on, the bar slowly emptied. By midnight, Pinnelli and the three men with him, were all that remained. Their booze-filled conversation became increasingly more heated.

While Dick sat at the end of the bar watching TV, an argument erupted between Pinnelli and the man sitting opposite him. Glaring at Pinnelli, the man yelled, "You're full of shit, Pinnelli! It can't be coming from the Rockman. He hasn't been around here for years."

"Wise up, you son of a bitch!" Pinnelli shot back with a murderous look in his eye. "That damned silver didn't show up at this bar until the Rockman came back."

"That may be so," the balding man yelled right back, "but that doesn't prove a thing."

Not giving any ground, Pinnelli asked, "What the hell do you think he was doing for money during the depression? While the rest of us were nearly starving, he was walking around in new clothes and driving new cars."

He could have been running bootleg whiskey like everyone else around here," one of the other men chimed in.

Wall of Silver

"Bootleg whiskey, my ass!" Pinnelli yelled. "Tell that to my brother Clarence, and he'd tell you that you don't know what your talking about!"

In a sarcastic tone of voice, one of the men asked Pinnelli, "If you know so damned much about the Rockman, then why don't you tell us how he made his money back then?"

Glaring at the man, his face red from yelling, Pinnelli crushed out his cigarette and told what he knew: "It happened in the fall of 1927. Me and my brother Clarence were living in Hancock. In the middle of the night, I was awakened by a loud knock on the door. When I went to the door and opened it, there were two tough-looking guys standing on the porch. One of them asked me if Clarence Pinnelli lived there. After I woke Clarence and he introduced himself, one of the men asked him if he wanted to make some extra money. Somehow the guy must have found out that Clarence was a diesel mechanic because he offered him $200 to repair a diesel engine. The guy told him it was an emergency. It turned out they had a boat that was having engine trouble and they were on a tight schedule. Out of work like most of us, Clarence got dressed, got his tool box, and left with the two guys."

Pausing just long enough to light another cigarette, Pinnelli looked through his half-closed eye at the others sitting at the table. Certain that he had their attention, he said, "I've never told this story before because those guys threatened Clarence and warned him to keep his mouth shut." After a long draw from his glass of beer, Pinnelli continued with his story: "About three hours later my brother returned with $200 and what looked like a piece of coal." Pinnelli paused, anticipating questions.

Crystal-Encased Silver

Puzzled by the coal, one of the men asked, "Where did they take him?"

"To the Dollar Bay Docks, where a steel barge was tied up. They were loading ore barrels onto the barge when one of them split open and spilled pieces of ore near the engine that Clarence was working on. When Clarence heard Jake Stockard's voice, he slipped a piece of ore into his tool box."

Pinnelli obviously had the attention of his band of ruffians and questions started coming fast.

"What the hell was Stockard doing there?"

"By the looks of it, Clarence thought he was helping the dock workers load the barrels onto the barge," Pinnelli answered.

"Did he see your brother?" someone asked.

"Clarence said he stayed out of sight."

"What kind of ore was it?" one of the men asked.

"It was unusually dark in color. At first we thought it was coal, but after I beat it with a hammer we found out it was silver ore."

"Did your brother happen to notice how many barrels were loaded aboard the barge?"

"He said he counted sixteen or seventeen barrels."

Dumfounded, the three men fell silent. Surprised as well, Dick was pretending that he didn't hear Pinnelli's story as he continued to watch TV. Minutes later, the silence was broken when one of the men asked, "Are you sure it was silver ore?"

Pinnelli said that it appeared to be and confessed to staking out Jake's farm and following his truck a number of times, even tracking him down by the cliffs.

Wall of Silver

His brother was too scared to join him because the men had threatened to kill him if he told anyone what he saw that night.

One of the men removed his weather-beaten hat, scratched his head, and said in a grating voice, "One thing is for sure, if there was silver in this area, Stockard would be the one to know where it was. He knew more about rocks and minerals than anyone else."

For the first time that night, the four men found something they all agreed on. When the group finally left, Dick swept the tavern, and thought about the intriguing story he had just heard. From the hostile tone of his voice, he felt that Pinnelli was still capable of killing to get what he wanted in spite of his age. Fearful that Jake might be exposing himself to danger, Dick decided to tell him all that he heard.

Fear Of
The Past

The next morning after having breakfast with Barb and the kids, Dick left the house with his money pouch and headed for Traprock Valley. When he reached the valley, it was still blanketed by a heavy layer of fog. Incapable of seeing the outline of the farmhouse until he was nearly upon it, Dick parked on the side of the house next to Jake's pickup and knocked on the front door. When there was no answer or movement inside, he left the porch and scanned the barely visible barn and outbuildings. Unable to see any signs of Jake, Dick called out, "Hey Jake! Are you out there?" His voice carried through the fog-shrouded property, and moments later the dark outline of a figure appeared on the end of the barn. Uncertain if it was Jake, he called out, "Is that you Jake?"

"Yeah, it's me," his familiar voice boomed. "Come over here."

With the money bag stuffed in his pocket, Dick headed for the barn. As he got closer to Jake, he noticed that he was dressed in a long black rubber apron and was wearing rubber gloves. When he got close enough to speak to him without yelling, Dick said, "I thought you said that Vern Parker was renting your farm?"

Jake answered that the Parkers were living in the guest house until he could make up his mind if he was going to sell the farm. Jake asked, "Did you have any trouble with Pinnelli after I left?"

Dick said he thought he might start a fight but that two of his comrades calmed him down. He said, "He may be an old son of a bitch, but I sure as hell wouldn't want to tangle with him."

"Oh, he's bad all right," Jake agreed. "When I worked with him years ago, he was suspected of killing three men underground and making it look like an accident."

"That doesn't surprise me at all," Dick said. "When I saw he was carrying a knife on his hip, I stayed clear of him."

Craving a cigarette but not wanting to smoke in the barn, Jake took off his gloves and motioned Dick to sit down on a bench next to the open door. After both men lit their cigarettes, Jake asked, "Do you have any idea what Pinnelli was shooting off his mouth about?"

"The silver that we've been selling in the bar."

"I assume from what I heard Pinnelli say to you he doesn't believe you found it. Right?"

"He thinks it belongs to you." Dick said.

Interested in learning how much Pinnelli knew about his past, Jake asked, "Did you hear anything that would back up his claim?"

"Well, I was sitting close enough to hear all he had to say, and he told a mighty strange story," Dick said.

Fear Of The Past

Looking sombre, Jake asked Dick if he cared to tell him the story.

Dick retold the story of Pinnelli's brother Clarence and the barge.

Jake exclaimed, "That's how the son of a bitch found out! I remember that night well, now that you've mentioned it. But how in the hell did he ever figure out that it was silver?"

"According to Pinnelli, Clarence stole a piece of what he thought was coal and took it home in his tool box. But, it was Nick himself who discovered it was oxidized ore," Dick said.

"Damn his hide!" Jake cursed. "That's why he was tracking me when I was hauling it out from the cliffs."

"Were you aware he was following you?" Dick asked.

Jake said he saw Nick Pinnelli but thought he was poaching deer because of the rifle he was carrying. He was even more aware now that, if Pinnelli followed all of his movements, when the time was right, he could have easily sealed Jake in the mine.

Dick said, "If that's the risk you have to take to get more silver to sell, forget it!"

"Good! When he discovers that it isn't coming from the cliffs, it will blow his mind," Jake said gleefully.

Confused, Dick asked, "What do you mean?"

"Because I've got it stashed in the barn," Jake revealed.

Ecstatic, Dick inquired, "Just how much do you have?"

Jake said it was enough to keep Dick selling for a long time and he would show him just how much as soon as they finished the job Jake had started, cleaning the rest of the silver.

Dick followed Jake past the cattle feeder and milking stalls that lined the outer walls of both sides of the barn and asked if he thought people would ask questions if more silver continues to appear in the tavern.

Jake said he did at first, but after hearing what Dick said about the Pinnellis, he didn't "give a damn anymore." He added, "Besides, we aren't breaking the law as long as nobody finds out where it originally came from. And at my age, I don't intend to haul any more of it from the mine."

Dick continued to express his concern about the people the silver could bring into the area asking questions: "If more silver shows up at the bar, there's going to be one hell of a lot of prospectors out by the cliffs turning over every rock and digging all over the place, plus it's just possible that one of them might find your mine. If that happened, the mining company that owns the land could come looking for you."

Aware that Dick was right, Jake quizzed him, "On what grounds?"

"I'm not familiar with the laws of mining," Dick conceded, "but I seriously doubt that there is any statute of limitations on jumping patented mining claims. There is also the possibility that the government might be interested in what you did with the silver you loaded on the barge, and how and to whom it was sold, especially now that Pinnelli's shooting off his mouth."

"Shit! You can't be serious! All of that took place more than forty years ago!" Jake exclaimed.

"You and I know that," Dick replied, "but as far as the government is concerned, you could have been selling it as late as 1964."

Jake asked how they could prove anything and Dick said there was only one way and that was if someone

Fear Of The Past

found the mine along with something that proved Jake had been there.

Faced with the possibility of such a scenario, Jake wiped his sweating face and neck with his handkerchief. Then, as his fingers brushed the silver chain that held a key around his neck, he thought of the steel box he'd hidden in the mine. Suddenly confident that no one would ever find the mine that had remained hidden for well over a hundred years before he found it, Jake brushed his fears aside and said, "Come on! Let's get the silver cleaned so we can get out of here."

When they reached the stall where a lit Coleman lantern hung from a post, Jake placed a hand on Dick's shoulder and said, "You worry too much. The important thing is that you're making money."

As the two men joked around and laughed, Jake slipped on his rubber gloves and motioned Dick to sit down beside him on an old milking stool. After he instructed him on how to wrap thin copper wire around the pieces of blackened silver ore so that they could be dipped into the nitric acid, Jake handed Dick a surgical mask to put on: "It's better than holding a handkerchief to your nose."

After each piece gleamed like a newly minted silver coin, they cut the wire and allowed it to fall into a bucket of cold water.

Sometime later, after the last specimen was cleaned and the lingering acid fumes had drifted out of the opened window at the rear of the stall, the two men removed their masks and set them aside. After glancing at the soaking silver, Jake took off his gloves and apron and said, "Let's let the silver soak for a few minutes while I show you where it came from." He added, "I hope you understand, son, what I'm about to show you hasn't been seen by anyone except me. I expect you will keep it confidential."

"I understand, Jake!" Dick said, "It will never get past me."

Jake led Dick into a building filled with all sorts of farm equipment. Wondering why Jake had brought him there, Dick looked around the cluttered room, and asked why they were there.

Pleased by this reaction, Jake chuckled and said, "This is where the silver's coming from."

"You've got to be kidding!" Dick said. "There's nothing but junk in here."

"That's exactly what I hoped people would think when I hid it here," Jake said as he handed Dick the lantern. After tossing aside pieces of junk, Jake pushed away the thick layer of straw with his foot until a wooden plank floor was exposed. He then got down on his hands and knees and pulled sections of planking loose and set them aside. When the opening was big enough to look into, Jake took the lantern from Dick, held it over the open pit and told him to take a look.

On his hands and knees, Dick looked into the partially exposed large pit and saw a familiar sparkle of crystal. Shocked he asked, "Is all that silver ore?"

"You bet it is!" Jake affirmed.

As they headed back towards the cleaning stall, Dick noted, "It's amazing that someone hasn't found that pit after all these years."

"Yeah, even Treasury Agents couldn't find it."

Surprised by Jake's remark, Dick asked, "What were Treasury Agents doing here?"

Fear Of The Past

Jake explained his encounter with the two Treasury Agents and the resulting charges, which he was able to escape by way of the "collector's items" loophole.

"You were lucky they didn't find that silver we just looked at; otherwise, they could have put you away for a long time," Dick said.

Jake agreed and Dick continued, "That same law wouldn't apply today because in 1964 silver was removed as a monetary metal."

When Jake asked about the statute of limitations, Dick said, "I suspect you could get into trouble if someone could prove you were illegally selling it before 1964."

"Hell! I'm too old to worry about such things." Jake said.

Once inside the house and seated at the kitchen table, the two men talked over sandwiches and beer. Jake asked what Dick took in from selling the silver in the tavern and he said, "Would you believe $2,356?"

"That's great!"

Dick asked why Jake didn't sell all of the silver ore in the barn, and Jake said it was because he got scared when he found out what they were doing with it. He pushed himself away from the table and left the room. He returned to the kitchen a few minutes later with a roll of coins, and tossed it to Dick saying, "Take a look at those coins, and tell me what you see." Opening the paper-wrapped roll of half dollars, Dick poured a few into the palm of his hand and studied the slightly tarnished coins. Being somewhat of a coin collector himself, he took one of the coins, inspected it closely, and remarked, "What am I supposed to be looking for?"

Jake said, "Check closely, and see if you can find anything wrong with them?"

Wall of Silver

After looking at the coins again, Dick said, "Outside of being a 1934 standing Liberty Half Dollar, uncirculated and slightly tarnished, I see nothing unusual."

Grinning his famous grin, Jake said, "All those coins are counterfeit."

Flabbergasted, Dick blurted out, "You've got to be shitting me! They look real to me."

"They are better than the God-damned mint made, because those suckers are .999 fine, and the mint's are only .920 content."

Astounded, Kellogg asked, "What were they paying you an ounce?"

"A guarantee of thirty-five cents."

"Jumping Jesus! At that rate, the bastards were making a clear profit of sixty-five cents an ounce by just counterfeiting common date coins. No wonder they got greedy." Dick said.

Jake said he figured they just wanted to have it both ways. "If they found out where I was getting the silver and got rid of me, they could have bought the property for a song back then and opened up a legitimate mining operation. There's nobody up here that would have cared or known the difference if I suddenly came up missing."

"I wonder why Fattori didn't go along with the program?" Dick mused.

"I've thought about that for years," Jake answered. "I guess he just wasn't the type of man who would go along with a murder, especially of someone he knew."

"Fattori must have known he'd be a marked man if they ever found out that he warned you."

"I'm sure he was well aware of that," Jake answered.

Dick asked if Jake knew where Fattori had gone and Jake told him what Fattori had said the last time they

Fear Of The Past

were together–that he was going to live with his brother in Canada.

"Did you ever have the feeling that you were being watched after Fattori warned you?" Dick asked.

"I sure did! But I never gave them a chance to find out where I got the silver. I shut everything down, and decided to take my rock and mineral collection on the road."

Dick brought up Jake's trip to England: "Did you find anything that led you to who discovered the mine?"

Without answering, Jake left the room and returned a few minutes later with a large, aging manila envelope in his hand. After removing the tape from the end of it, he handed it to his friend and said, "Can you stay for supper?"

"Sure!" he replied, "is there anything I can do?"

"Why don't you go into the living room, settle down and build a fire while I drive uptown to pick up a couple of steaks and some beer."

Reading Of
The Journal

After building a fire, Dick settled down in an easy chair near the fireplace. As he held the envelope in his hands, he noticed it was addressed to Jake. Its postal cancellation date was June 3, 1936. In the upper left hand corner a return address read: Richard Stone, Rural Route 2, Box 52, Sault Ste. Marie, Michigan.

Inside the envelope he found photocopies of Sabin Stone's original journals, papers and a crude map detailing the mine's whereabouts. As the smell of the burning pine logs filled the room, Dick began to read. When he finished reading Sabin Stone's papers, he breathed a deep sigh and muttered, "This is just too incredible!"

After he slipped the historic file back into the envelope, he lay back, stared into the fire, and thought about the many questions he had.

When Jake returned with a bag of groceries and saw that Dick had finished reading the journals, he said, "Well, what do you think of it?"

Wall of Silver

As both men walked into the kitchen Dick answered, "It's mighty interesting. Is the Wall of Silver Mine the same mine that you found?"

Unpacking the groceries, Jake answered, "I've had almost thirty-five years to reflect on that question, and my gut feeling is that they're one in the same."

"How did you come to find the mine when no one else had found it in over 150 years?"

After Jake opened two beers and handed one to Dick, he said, "It's a long story. Let's go sit by the fire and I'll tell you about it."

The two men took seats opposite each other and Jake started his story: "Like I said before, it was 1927. I was unemployed like most people up here back then. In an attempt to pick up some extra money, I decided to go prospecting that summer for rare rocks and minerals with the hope of selling them to the wealthy collectors I knew. I packed all my gear into my pickup truck and headed for the cliffs."

After giving a brief history of the Cliff region, Jake added, "Back then Cliff Drive was just a narrow two-track dirt road that serviced the Cliff Mine and logging interests in that area. At the time that region was covered with dense forest and had numerous logging roads meandering through it, one of which extended, within a very short distance, to the base of the cliffs."

Thinking he knew the barely visible dirt road, Dick asked, "Is that the one that ends a short distance from the volcanic ridge?"

"That's right," Jake answered.

An amateur prospector himself in his spare time, Dick asked if there was a reason that area was prime hunting for rare specimens.

Terrain within Township 58 North-Range 31 West, Section 28 and 29 where the Wall of Silver Mine is located. Photo taken by the Author.

Wall of Silver

"It's because, from time to time, the facings of the cliff would collapse. When they did, they sometimes exposed previously hidden rocks and minerals." Jake continued with his story: "After I explored that area for the better part of the day without finding anything of interest, I was just about ready to leave when my eyes caught sight of something that sparkled in the sunlight. When I picked up a moss-covered rock with crystals sticking out of it, I noticed that it felt heavier than common rock. So, I scratched its surface with the blade of my knife and found that it was a chunk of silver ore. It was the only one I found but something strange happened that night after I decided to camp out."

"It was just about dark. I had set up camp near the base of the cliff and built a fire. As I sat on my bedroll watching the smoke rise in the still night air, it strangely swirled and dispersed to the south. Thinking it was rather strange, I threw more green branches on the fire and watched it closely. When I saw the smoke disperse on about a forty-five-degree angle and again drift to the south, I traced a column of air coming from between the rocks left at the base of the cliff by a previous rock slide. I removed rocks from the slide until I exposed a wall of stacked rotting timbers that were cut to fit the opening. After I removed the timbers, I found myself staring into a gaping black hole large enough to accommodate a huge grizzly bear."

Jake took a drink of his beer and continued, "Rather than enter at night what appeared to be a tunnel, I tied a rope to the handle of my lantern and lowered it down the hole. As the lantern skidded down what looked like a fifteen-degree slope, it disappeared from sight as it rounded a slight bend. From the size of the tunnel, the lack of diggings on the surface, and the strong draft coming from the hole, I definitely figured it to be a tunnel of some sort."

"Damned!" Dick exclaimed. "Weren't you afraid of entering it?"

"You bet I was," said Jake without shame. "I gave it a lot of thought before I did because I had the strange feeling it might be trapped." Next he told about throwing the boulder down the tunnel and springing the bear trap. "After I reached bottom and got to my feet, I was surprised that I could stand up with room to spare."

Dick said, "According to Stone's Journal he was a very tall man; do you think that's why you had room to spare?"

Jake nodded and said, "As I stood there planning my next move, my attention was drawn to finding the source of air and the sound of roaring water in the distance. Before I left the front of the mine, I noticed that a cave-in had taken place and sealed off the main entrance. That's when I knew that I had entered the mine through an escape tunnel."

"I wonder why nobody ever saw the caved-in entrance from outside the mine," Dick said.

"Because it's completely hidden beneath a rock slide that took place later, when a portion of the cliff collapsed in that area." Jake explained.

Responding to Dick's question if the mine was dry, Jake said, "In spite of the sound of fast moving water, the mine was relatively free of dampness. It turned out that the early miners had broken through the end of the tunnel and into a huge cavern that contained a good-sized water-fall and a large whirlpool at its base."

"Did you find any more traps in the mine?"

Wall of Silver

"Fortunately I didn't."

"How strange! Could you see daylight?"

"None whatsoever!" Jake said and added another log to the fire. "From the cavern I headed back through the main tunnel and followed it until it ended to the south where considerable mining had taken place. It was there, I found, that the early miners encountered a solid mass of silver." Jake paused, but Dick was at a loss for words.

"When I headed back towards the front of the mine, I entered a tunnel that meandered in a southerly direction until it widened out into a large area that was supported by numerous pillars that had been left in place. It was there that I found what appeared to be the extension of the same mass of silver that I had encountered at the rear of the mine."

Dick found his voice and exclaimed, "My God! They must have found the Mother Lode that everyone has been searching for all these years."

"I don't know about that, but it sure as hell is the biggest mass of silver I've ever seen."

Astonished by the magnitude of Jake's discovery, Dick asked, "What did it feel like finding something so valuable?"

After contemplating for a few moments, Jake replied. "At first I thought of the potential of being independently wealthy but then I felt an overwhelming need to tell the world about it."

Dick shook his head in dismay and said, "I can understand that, but you could have lost it all."

"Yes, I know," Jake replied. "But I thought of becoming famous for having found a part of unwritten history."

Realizing that Jake would have liked to tell the world of his discovery without losing it, Dick suggested,

Reading Of The Journal

"Why don't you take some movies inside the mine, and write a book?"

Jake said he had thought of doing that but it would take a crew to do it right and he wasn't any good at writing. He asked Dick about his writing skills.

"I've done considerable writing in my day, but I'd have to see the mine in person and take pictures before I could write about it," he answered.

That was just the encouragement Jake needed. Excited, he said, "The best time is during the spring rains because there shouldn't be any poachers wandering the woods."

Jake left the room briefly and returned with the envelope containing the journal along with the roll of half dollars. He handed them to Dick and said, "You might as well take these if you're going to write that book. Don't let anyone see them except your wife, and as far as paying you to write this story, I'll take care of that when we go down into the mine."

Selling The Tavern

By the Spring of 1973, the once-full pit in the barn was nearly empty. When the law passed allowing eighteen year olds to drink, Dick, concerned about his future, catered to the young college crowd and also brought in rock bands for entertainment. Even though business was good, he became disenchanted with the bar business and all its pressures. Secretly, he had serious thoughts of selling the business.

His chance finally came on a Sunday morning as he was dressing to go trout fishing with Jake out at the farm. The phone rang; it was long distance. A man's voice asked, "Is this Dick Kellogg, the owner of the Sportsman Bar?"

"Yes it is! What can I do for you?"

"My name is Tom Keating with Investments Unlimited, and I have a client who is interested in buying your place. Are you interested in selling it?" Obviously,

Wall of Silver

Mr. Keating was familiar with the bar because he made an offer right then.

Kellogg asked, "How soon do you have to know?"

"Within ninety days," the agent replied.

"Fine! Give me a call about then, and I'll let you know." Elated, but concerned about how Jake would react to the news, Dick finished dressing, gathered up his fishing gear, and left the house.

By the time he reached the farm, most of the fog had burned off in the valley, and it turned out to be a nice day. As Dick's noisy Jeep turned off the county road and onto the long driveway that led to the farm, Jake gathered up his fly rod and creel and walked off the porch to meet him as he pulled into the yard.

"Running late!" Jake kidded.

"I'd have been here sooner but I got a long distance call from downstate."

"I hope it wasn't bad news," Jake said as he watched Dick struggle into his waders.

"I guess you could say it was good news and bad news," Dick replied as both men cut across the field and headed for the river.

"Does it have anything to do with me?" Jake asked.

"Yeah, in a way, I guess you could say it does."

"Care to talk about it?" Jake asked as he approached a wind-fallen pine and motioned Dick to sit down beside him.

After taking a deep breath, Dick turned to Jake and said. "I've got some people interested in buying the tavern."

Caught completely by surprise, Jake exclaimed, "I had no idea you were even thinking of selling now that you're back on your feet."

Selling The Tavern

"I really wasn't, but I'm afraid I have no choice." Dick began to explain: "First of all, the silver in the barn is almost gone. Secondly, there are strong rumors in the state capital that the teenage drinking law might be repealed next year. If that happens, I'll be right back where I started before you came along and saved me from financial ruin."

Jake checked his fishing gear in silence before he spoke. Then he asked, "What are you going to do if you sell the tavern?"

"Go back to Lower Michigan because there's no other way to make a living up here."

"I thought you hated the city." Jake said. "Have you made any commitments?"

"No, I've got ninety days to think about it."

As they moved silently towards the river, Jake said, "Ya know, we've had many good times together. In the short time I've known you, you have become like the son I never had."

Dick was too astounded to speak.

At the river as they tied flies to their lines, Jake said, "If I could make it worth your while, would you stay in the Copper Country after you sold the tavern?"

"Maybe! What do you have in mind?"

"Would you be interested in working the mine with me and splitting the profits fifty/fifty?" Jake proposed.

Put at a loss for words by Jake's generosity and the fact that he was willing to share a secret that he had kept all his life, Dick asked, "But why? I'm sure you don't need the money."

Not the kind of man who found it easy to express his feelings, Jake grinned and said, "Let's just say I'd hate to lose my fishing partner."

Wall of Silver

Intrigued by Jake's offer, Dick asked, "Who would we sell the silver to?"

"You could open a rock shop in downtown Calumet, and tourists would be breaking down your front door."

"I'll let you know after I see what the mine looks like."

Elated, Jake remarked, "We should be able to go to the mine in about a couple of weeks."

Dick expressed concern about Pinnelli and his tribe following them, but Jake said he'd act as a decoy on the nights Dick hauled out ore.

"Do you think he's figured out where the silver's coming from that we've been selling in the bar?" Dick asked.

"I'm sure he's figured out by this time, that it's coming from some place on the farm."

"If that's the case, we better head for the mine before our supply runs out." Dick suggested.

"Our best bet is to go when the next major storm moves into the area." Jake said.

Dick asked what gear he needed. Jake said if he had a snowmobile outfit, that would be all he'd need. He said he would pick up all the lighting and other necessary supplies.

"Will it be cold in the mine?" Dick asked.

"Not really; it usually stays at a constant of about fifty degrees," Jake answered.

Dick asked if he should take a gun and Jake said, "Most definitely."

"How will I know for sure when were going?"

"I'll keep in close touch with the Weather Service to see when they predict the next batch of bad weather, and then I'll give you a call." Jake said.

"Do you think he'll attempt to follow us?"

"He sure as hell will if he spots any activity here on the farm."

Selling The Tavern

After the men finished a day of fishing, Dick left the farm and headed for home. When he told Barb about Jake's plans, she was definitely against Dick's going to the mine, and was emphatic that they should sell the tavern and leave the Copper Country.

Last Trip
To The Mine

A week later, after church, Dick and his two sons went to the Sportsman's Bar to fill the beer coolers.

When they entered the tavern, it looked like a tornado had blown through the interior. The many amusement machines were smashed and coins were scattered all over the floor. The gun rack that once held a number of antique guns was ripped off the wall and the guns were missing. In the far corner of the room, the display case that contained Jake's priceless specimen was smashed and the specimen was missing. A further inspection of the premises revealed that the rear service entrance door had been torn from the building, and all of the beer stock and liquor was missing. After the police investigated the break-in, nothing could be found to bring the culprits to justice.

Unable to afford the insurance to cover such a loss, the Kelloggs had to dip into their meager savings. As for

Wall of Silver

STATE OF MICHIGAN
DEPARTMENT OF STATE POLICE
Lansing

JENNIFER M. GRANHOLM
GOVERNOR

COL. TADARIAL J. STURDIVANT
DIRECTOR

NOV 2 4 2003

MR RICHARD KELLOGG
2837 NORTH THOMAS PLACE
TRAVERSE CITY, MI 49686-

RE: CR-31016-04

Dear MR KELLOGG:

The department of State Police has received your request for certain information and has processed it under the provisions of the Michigan Freedom of Information Act (FOIA), P.A. 442, of 1976, as amended.

The records which you have requested have been:

☐   Granted. The requested documents are ENCLOSED.

☐   Granted in part and denied in part. Portions of your request are exempt from disclosure based on provisions set forth in the Act. (See comments on the back of this letter.) The granted documents are ENCLOSED. Under the FOIA, Section 10 (a copy of which is enclosed), you have the right to appeal or to a judicial review of the denial.

☒   Denied. (See comments on the back of this letter.) Under the FOIA, Section 10 (a copy of which is enclosed), you have the right to appeal or to a judicial review of the denial.

☐   Your request for photographs has been sent to the Michigan State Police Photo Lab for processing. They will respond to your request within ten (10) business days.

Please pay the amount of $ ―0― to the address below. The check or money order should be made payable to the **STATE OF MICHIGAN.** To ensure proper credit, please **enclose a copy of this letter with your payment.**

If you have questions concerning this matter, please feel free to contact our office at the address below, and enclose a copy of this correspondence.

Sincerely,

Linda Ortiz
Assistant FOIA Coordinator
Michigan State Police

GENERAL OFFICE BUILDING • 7150 HARRIS DRIVE • LANSING. MICHIGAN 48913
www.michigan.gov • (517) 322-5531

My attempt to obtain records and investigation reports of violation of the law that took place during my period of ownership of the Sportsman's Bar during the years of 1968 through 1973.

Due to the passing of more than thirty years and the destruction of my home it was impossible for me to provide the exact dates of when these incidents took place. As a result when I contacted the State of

DENIAL OF RECORDS:
Denial is based on the following provision(s) of the Freedom of Information Act. MCL 15.243, Sec. 13(1). (All that apply will be checked.)

☐ (a)   Information of a personal nature where the public disclosure of the information would constitute a clearly unwarranted invasion of an individual's privacy.
☐ telephone number(s)   ☐ address(es)   ☐ date(s) of birth   ☐ physical characteristics   ☐ driver license number(s)
☐ other _____

☐ (b)   Investigating records compiled for law enforcement purposes, but only to the extent that disclosure would do any of the following:
☐ (i)   Interfere with law enforcement proceedings.
☐ (ii)   Deprive a person of the right to a fair trial or impartial administrative adjudication
☐ (iii) Constitute an unwarranted invasion of personal privacy.
☐ (iv)   Disclose the identity of a confidential source, or if the record is compiled by a law enforcement agency in the course of a criminal investigation, disclose confidential information furnished only by a confidential source.
☐ (vi)   Endanger the life or physical safety of law enforcement personnel.

☐ (d)   Records or information specifically described and exempted from disclosure by statute.
Statute: _____

☐ (m)   Communications and notes within a public body or between public bodies of an advisory nature to the extent that they cover other than purely factual materials and are preliminary to a final agency determination of policy or action.

☐ (n)   Records of law enforcement communication codes, or plans for deployment of law enforcement personnel, that if disclosed would prejudice a public body's ability to protect the public.

☐ (s)   Unless the public interest in disclosure outweighs the public interest in nondisclosure in the particular instance, public records of a law enforcement agency, the release of which would do any of the following:
☐ (i)   Identify or provide a means of identifying an informer.
☐ (ii)   Identify or provide a means of identifying a law enforcement undercover officer or agent or a plain clothes officer as a law enforcement officer or agent.
☐ (viii) Identify or provide a means of identifying a person as a law enforcement officer, agent, or informer.
☐ (ix)   Disclose personnel records of law enforcement agencies.

☐ (u)   Records of a public body's security measures, including security plans, security codes and combinations, passwords, passes, keys, and security procedures, to the extent that the records relate to the ongoing security of the public body.

☐ (w)   Information or records that would disclose the social security number of any individual.

☐   Your request is denied under the authority of Section 13(1)(a) above. However, if you provide a notarized, signed release of information from the individual to whom the records pertain, you will receive that information to which the individual signing the release is entitled.

☐   The documents do not exist within this department. _____

☒   Based on the information you provided, we are unable to locate any records pertaining to the incident you described. In order for us to continue processing your request, please comply with the following items. To ensure proper handling of your request, please include a copy of this letter with your response.
☐ Specific location (i.e. city, county.)
☒ Michigan State Police incident number
☐ Names of those involved in the incident
☒ Specific dates (i.e., date of Incident)
☐ Name of driver and their birth date or driver license number
☐ Date of birth

☐   The report you have requested has not yet been completed and filed. Please contact this office in 30 days to request that the report be retrieved.

Additional Comments:

Michigan–Criminal Justice Information Center for possible copies of the above requested reports, I was denied this request.

I truly wished I could have gotten those documents as I feel it would have added more credence to this incredible story.

The Author

Wall of Silver

Jake's loss, he brushed it off with the remark, "Don't worry about it; wait till they try to sell it and find out it's not worth facing prison."

A short time after the robbery, Barbara Kellogg picked up the mail at the Kearsarge Post Office and was horrified when she read the following letter. Made up of cutout pieces of print and glued to a page of common stationary, it read: "Kelloggs - Leave Copper Country or Die!"

After a lengthy investigation by the Postal Service proved futile, Dick obtained a concealed weapon permit and began to carry a gun. Through the days that followed, Dick's fear for his family led to such severe paranoia that his wife had him committed to a Psychiatric Department at a Marquette hospital. After weeks of intensive treatment, he was released. With Jake's mine constantly on his mind, he called Jake and asked, "Do you still want to take me to the mine?"

Surprised to hear Dick's voice, Jake asked, "When did you get released?"

"Yesterday, they gave me a clean bill of health."

Jake said they'd make the trip to the mine the next time the Weather Service issued a forecast for bad weather.

It was only a week later when Jake called Dick and said, " Just checked with the weather station and I was told severe storms are expected to be moving into the area by tomorrow night. Can you be ready?"

"Sure can! Keep in touch," Dick answered.

The barometer fell all the next day; by nightfall warnings were up on the big lake, and by late evening, a line of severe thunderstorms had moved into the area. Whipped up by high winds, trees were uprooted and

Last Trip To The Mine

power lines were downed. To make matters worse, heavy rains had washed out roads and widespread flooding was being reported.

Fearing they would be trapped by the storm, people frequenting places that were normally open late, scurried away early for the safety of their homes.

Sportsman's Bar was no exception. Soon after the last customer left the tavern, Dick locked the doors and turned out the outside lights. Concerned about the intensity of the storm and the fact that they had plans of venturing out in it, Dick turned on the radio and tuned it to the local station that gave updates on the weather in the area.

Not long after he had finished counting the day's receipts and settled on the bar stool nearest the phone, the sound of music was interrupted by a man's voice. "Attention! The National Weather Service warns that another line of severe storms is moving into the Keweenaw, accompanied by high winds. It is expected that additional rains will bring the Trap Rock River to flood stage and cause extensive washing out of roads in the high country. Stay tuned to this station for further updates."

No sooner had Dick turned off the radio when the phone rang. It was Jake. Over the sound of thunder in the background, he asked, "Have you shut down yet?"

After a short conversation the two men decided they would still go to the mine. Jake would drive to the tavern where Dick would be waiting in the dark. Jake was to flash his lights and Dick would meet him at the back door.

A short time later Jake was crossing the Trap Rock River; it was barely a foot below flood stage. Keeping a

Wall of Silver

close lookout to see if he was being followed, Jake pulled into the empty Kearsarge Store parking lot and watched the nearby highway. Certain that he hadn't been followed, he continued on until he reached the tavern. Finding the parking lot empty except for Dick's Jeep, he flashed his lights and pulled to a stop at the back door.

Moments later, Dick emerged. Dressed in all-weather clothing and a rain poncho, he threw the rest of his gear into the back of the truck and got inside. Visibly excited, he looked at Jake and asked, "Did you see anyone?"

"Not a soul!"

As the two men headed north on U.S.41, they scanned the side roads for parked cars. Finding none, they continued farther north and passed Cliff Drive, where the mine was located. Satisfied that they weren't being followed, Jake doubled back and headed for the mine. When they reached the barely visible logging road near Seneca Lake, Jake turned to the west and headed for the cliffs.

The more than twenty years since Jake had last traveled the two-track had taken their toll. It was overgrown with thick scrub. He pulled to a stop and said, "It looks like this is the end of the line!"

"How much farther is it?" Dick asked.

Recognizing a huge cedar on his left, Jake guessed, "About another 200 yards."

After strapping on their backpacks and donning their hard hats with the battery-powered lamps, they left the truck and entered the thick brush.

By the time they reached their destination the rain had stopped and, except for an occasional flash of distant lightning and the sound of thunder, it was quiet.

Last Trip To The Mine

As Jake shined the bright beam of his powerful Maxi-Lite onto a large century-old pine, he exclaimed, "This is it!"

There was no sign that the area had been disturbed. Had Jake not described the site in previous conversations, Dick would have overlooked it as being a place of any importance.

Visibly anxious, Jake moved quickly to a rock pile near the base of the cliff and began to remove rocks and set them aside. Dick joined him and they soon exposed the wall of stacked railroad ties. No words were spoken as Jake checked the numbered heads on the spikes. When he was satisfied that they were in proper order, he turned to Dick and said, "It looks like the mine is still our secret!"

Overcome by the moment, Dick muttered, "This is hard to believe."

"Yeah! I still get chills down my spine, even though I've done this many times in the past." When the first timber was removed, Jake noted, "There's definitely less air flowing from the mine; something must have changed. There may have been a cave-in of some sort!"

After all the timbers were removed, Dick looked into the tunnel and gasped. When Jake turned to him, he asked, "Do you think you can handle it?"

Surprised by the smoothness of the base of the tunnel, Dick asked, "Why is it so smooth?"

"My guess is it's that way from the steel skids on the ore sleds that the early miners used."

Still apprehensive about going down the tunnel, Dick watched Jake as he slipped into knee pads, elbow pads and leather gloves. Before Jake backed into the tunnel, he turned on the lamp on his hard hat, looked up at Dick and asked, "Are you going to make the journey?"

"Yeah! I'll be ready in a few seconds."

"Good! After I reach the bottom and check things out, I'll pull on the rope twice. That's when you come down."

Dick nodded and said, "I've got it!"

With the end of the rope tied to the bottom timber, Jake backed into the tunnel. His heart pounding wildly, Dick watched as Jake went out of sight. Less than ten minutes later, when he felt the tug on the rope, Dick backed into the tunnel. Suddenly there was silence. No longer could he hear the sound of the wind and the occasional rumble of thunder. The only sound he could hear was the pounding in his chest. Relieved when he felt the touch of Jake's hand on his back, and Jake's pulling him to his feet, Dick remained silent as he looked around. Jake had already lit a number of candles in the front portion of the mine. Dick slowly looked around and muttered softly, "God this is scary!"

"Do you still want to continue?" Jake asked.

"Yes, I'll be all right," Dick answered. When he regained his composure, he asked, "Did you find the answer to the reduced flow of air?"

Jake explained that there had been a cave-in at the north end of the rear crosscut tunnel, where the early miners had broken through, and the air flow was almost half what it once was.

Dick asked, "Do we have to worry about it?"

"No!" Jake replied. "The rest of the tunnel looks solid."

When Dick's flashlight beam shined on a large pile of neatly stacked potato sacks in the front of the mine, he asked, "What are those?"

Last Trip To The Mine

"Bags of silver ore."

Noticing that the twenty-pound sacks were only partially filled, Dick asked, "How much do they weigh?"

Jake said each weighed between forty and fifty pounds. He said he put the ore into sacks to make it easier to transport it on an ore sled and then later in the truck.

"Boy! It sure looks like silver is heavier than potatoes," Dick said.

Jake laughed and asked, "Have you ever had the opportunity of lifting a bag of one thousand silver dollars?"

"Yes! On a couple of occasions. Why do you ask?"

"Because it will give you some kind of an idea on the weight of silver."

Dick asked, "How much does a bag of one thousand silver dollars weigh?"

"In avoirdupois weight based on sixteen ounces to the pound, a bag would weigh about sixty-four pounds."

Curious, Dick removed some ore from the stope and placed it on a scale that Jake had rigged up. After loading it with sixty-four pounds, he compared it to one of the already weighed potato sacks and said, "Jesus! Jake, this ore is very close to being pure silver!"

When Dick spotted what looked like a children's toboggan with copper sheathing covering its bottom, he asked, "Is that what you called an ore sled?"

Jake grinned and answered, "That's one of my earlier models. I tried numerous configurations until I came up with the most efficient."

Still astounded by the amount of ore that Jake had hauled to the surface, Dick asked, "How many bags of ore could you haul to the surface with the toboggan?"

"On my best day, I managed to haul about four hundred pounds to the surface."

Wall of Silver

"That must have been awfully hard work," Dick said.

Jake said that it was so hard he almost called it quits until he figured out how to use his truck to pull the ore to the surface. He said he used his truck to push the many boulders aside that fell from the higher elevations until he could get to within ten feet of the tunnel opening. Then he used a dock dolly to pull the ore up.

A short distance away, Jake located what looked like a dolly for moving refrigerators and other heavy objects and said, "After I reworked this dolly and put larger wheels on it, I'd lay it on its back, and, with a wooden pallet on it, I could load it with ten sacks and pull it to the surface without putting any strain on the truck."

"How much of a load could you haul with your truck?"

"It had a one-ton capacity, so I usually loaded it to only about a thousand pounds."

Dick asked how long the mining season was and Jake said it began just after the snow was out of the high country and ended when the snow came back in late October.

"Do you think we could still work the mine?" Dick asked.

"Not after seeing how much the logging road is blocked by heavy undergrowth, and, with the increase of traffic on the highway, I doubt that we could get in and out of here without being eventually seen," Jake answered.

Jake took Dick on a complete tour of the mine, during which Dick took numerous thirty-five millimeter slides. The tour ended at the base of a support pillar in the wall of silver area.

As Jake dug at the base of a support pillar with a rock wedge, Dick asked, "What are you looking for?"

"A steel box that contains a ledger on all my silver sales to Fattori."

Last Trip To The Mine

As Dick held the flashlight, Jake probed and dug for what seemed like a half hour. When he heard the sound of steel contacting steel, he stopped digging just long enough to clear away the broken rock exposing a large special built steel box. After clearing enough of the debris away, he reached for the heavy silver chain around his neck, removed a key, and unlocked the padlock. From a top tray, he removed what looked like a ledger about the size of an address book. Without saying a word, he scanned through it and put it into a pocket in his jumpsuit. From a pile of tightly stacked canvas bags, he removed two, handed them to Dick and said, "Here these are yours!"

Unaware of what the bags contained, Dick asked, "What for?"

"For writing the book you promised me!"

A closer look at the bags revealed that they contained twenty-five hundred dollars each in ten dollar gold coins. Stunned, Dick was lost for words and realized that he now had no choice but to write Jake's story. Eventually he said, "Jesus, Jake, you didn't have to pay me. I'd have done it for nothing."

"Nonsense! It's yours."

After Jake closed the box, locked it, and returned it to its hiding place, Dick asked, "Aren't you going to take it with you?"

"No! I really don't need it, and besides, it might come in handy as a bargaining tool if we're going to save the mine for future generations."

As he stared at the signatures of the early miners carved into the wall, Dick turned to Jake and asked, "Have you ever thought of carving your name on the wall?"

"Yes, but I changed my mind because I never thought I rightly deserved to have it there."

"Nonsense! If you hadn't rediscovered it, we wouldn't be here today."

Reluctantly, Jake agreed: "I suppose you're right."

Dick asked for a tool to carve with and Jake directed him to a tool box next to the ore sled, where he found a jeweler's tool. After carving Jake's full name and dating it, Dick turned to Jake and asked, "Well! What do you think of it?"

With tears in his eyes, Jake replied, "Thank you, Dick. It looks great!"

"Now, stand over here, and I'll get a picture of it."

As the two men did another tour of the large mined-out area, Dick asked, "Do you ever expect to return to this place?"

Visibly tired, Jake shook his head and answered, "At my age, I don't expect to get another chance."

"Aren't you planning on taking the gold with you?"

"No, I have no need for it!"

Dick was puzzled by the answer and said Jake could at least donate it to charity. Jake said he had thought about that many times but there would always be so many questions on how and where he got it.

Dick said, "That may be true, but it seems like an awful waste."

Jake said it wouldn't be if the gold could somehow be used to save the mine. Dick asked how much gold was remaining in the strong box and Jake said, less the five thousand he gave Dick, there remained thirty thousand in coins.

"My God, Jake! That's an awful lot of money, when you figure how much it would bring on the present gold

Last Trip To The Mine

market, and probably a lot more if the coins are sold as collector coins." Dick said.

Jake insisted he wanted the money used to save the mine for future generations and Dick said he would do all he could to see that wish come true.

Jake glanced at his watch, and said, "We'd better be getting to the surface because it will be dawn soon."

After all the candles were extinguished, Jake grabbed the toboggan and both men headed for the front of the mine. Before they went up, Jake loaded the two bags of gold coins onto the ore sled and it was pulled to the surface. On the surface, the rain had stopped and dawn was breaking in the east. After the entrance to the mine was concealed, Jake asked Dick, "Do you think you can find this place if necessary?"

Dick looked around him and said, "I believe I could."

On the way home, Jake asked, "Do you think you might want to work the mine and open a rock and mineral shop in Calumet?"

Dick said not after getting the letter threatening his family. He felt especially bad about it, he told Jake, since he had invested a lot of time and money in his new home. He had run for state representative of the district with the hope of changing things locally. And he had gone to Washington to have the area designated a "Depressed Manpower Region." He brought back a large government contract that would have provided the training and employment of 150 people but he never got it started because no one would rent one of the many vacant buildings to him. Jake said it was because all of the business people were afraid of the mining company. It was beginning to look like Dick was giving up on the Copper Country.

Wall of Silver

The letter above certifies that the author ran for election in 1970. Right: The picture used during his political campaign in the Copper Country.

Last Trip To The Mine

"Are you going to accept that offer you got on the tavern?" Jake asked.

"I'm afraid so," Dick sighed.

"When will you know for sure if they'll purchase it?"

"I'm going downstate next week with the family and will look over the offer then," Dick said.

Death Of A Legend

After making arrangements for someone to run the tavern while they were gone, the Kellogg family left for downstate.

One week later at his parents' home, Dick received a phone call from Vernon Parker informing him that Jake had died suddenly from a massive stroke only a few hours earlier. Stunned by the loss of his best friend, Dick left for the Copper Country that same evening.

When he arrived at the farm some twelve hours later, Vern met him at the door. With tears in his eyes Vernon reached out his hand and said, "I'm deeply sorry, Dick. His last words were to tell you that he loved you like the son he never had."

Through his own tear-filled eyes and barely able to speak, Dick asked, "Did he suffer much?"

Both men moved into the living room and sat down, Vern answered, "I'm quite sure he didn't, because, after he fell, he was only conscious long enough to ask me to give you that message."

"Do you have any idea what might have brought it on?"

"Well, he seemed all right this morning. He left the house right after I made his breakfast." Vern answered.

Dick asked if he knew where Jake went.

"When I went outside about lunchtime looking for him," Vern said, "I found him out by the barn splitting wood. I knew it would have been useless for me to tell him to stop, so I told him lunch was ready and returned to the house."

Dick continued questioning Vern, trying to understand what had happened. Vern said he noticed Jake having trouble keeping his balance when he returned to the house. When Vern suggested calling a doctor, Jake waved it off and headed for the den. Vern nervously lit a cigarette.

"How long was he in the den?" Dick asked.

Vern said about an hour. He checked on Jake and he seemed all right because he was writing something.

"What did he do next?" Dick asked.

"Well, that's what was very strange," the gaunt and slender middle-aged man recalled. "It was almost as if he knew he was going to die soon."

Surprised, Dick asked, "Why do you say that?"

"Because," he answered softly, "when he left the den, he was carrying that foot locker and strong box. He set them on the kitchen table, handed me a letter, and said, Be sure Dick gets this.'"

Vernon paused to pull himself together and then said, "After he returned to the den a few minutes later, I heard a stressful sound followed by a loud crash. When I went to the den, I found Jake lying facedown on the floor.

Death Of A Legend

When I turned him over, he opened his eyes briefly and told me how much he cared for you. He made me promise that you would get this letter and the things in the foot locker. He then lost consciousness and was dead by the time the ambulance got here."

"Did you know Jake well?" Dick asked.

Vern explained that yes, he did. They served together in World War Two in the Pacific and Vern credited Jake for helping him survive the Japanese death march in the Philippines.

Trying to fill in some gaps in what he knew about Jake, Dick asked, "Did you ever meet the woman he married in England?"

"No, I didn't. Jake was always such a private person."

"Did he have any heirs?" Dick asked.

Vern said he didn't know of any but suggested they see what Jake said in the letter he left for Dick.

After both men returned to the kitchen and sat down at the kitchen table, Dick picked up the envelope lying on the foot locker. After staring at the sealed document with his name on it, Dick opened it and took out a one-page letter along with Jake's last will and testament. In the simple will, drawn up a few days earlier by a local attorney, Jake left one-third of his large estate to the College of Mining that he had attended, along with all the rare specimens of silver from his rock and mineral collection. The will continued: "To my dearest friend, Vernon Parker and his lovely wife Freda, I leave this farm and all its contents. As for the balance of my estate, I have a foundation set up with my attorney to help the children of the world."

As Vernon watched in silence, Dick opened the envelope addressed to him, took out a handwritten note and read it in silence. In an unsteady handwriting it said, "To the son I never had, I know my days are numbered. Don't feel sorry for me, for I've had a good life and am only saddened by the fact that I couldn't tell the world of my discovery. Since I have already given you the journals and the roll of counterfeit half dollars, and the photographs of the tools in the mine, I am now giving you the key that will open the steel box that contained the gold coins and ledger that contains all my clandestine movements and the sale of silver." As he quickly paged through the log, a folded piece of paper fell onto the table: Made payable to a Chicago Bank and dated April 16, 1931, was a receipt from a cashiers check for $35,000 with Jacob Stockard as the remitter.

When he turned it over and read "P to G" (paper to gold) on the back in Jake's writing, he knew what it meant.

Jake's final request read: "I want to be cremated and my ashes scattered along the Greenstone Ridge. Godspeed! Jake."

Three days later and shortly after dawn, a helicopter at the county airport with Vernon Parker and Dick Kellogg aboard, headed for the Cliff Region. In a blazing sunrise the chopper lifted off and made a gentle climbing turn to the west.

Leave Or Die

Shortly after Jake's death, Dick sold the tavern to downstate interests and put his house up for sale. He still hoped that he could retrieve the steel box from the mine before he left the Copper Country. Alone, he decided to see if it was possible. He packed all the necessary gear for going underground and headed for the high country. Shortly after leaving his house, he sensed that he was being followed. After leading two men on a wild goose chase, he doubled back and later found their truck parked on a barely visible logging road. To his surprise, it didn't belong to Pinnelli or any of the men he hung around with. Convinced that it was a bad time to be going to the mine, he figured his only hope of returning to the mine hinged on the passing of considerable time.

It wasn't long before the Kelloggs sold their house to a geologist who worked for Homestake Mining Company. After secretly packing all their belongings, including two sealed wooden cases of silver specimens, Dick called a local moving company and arranged to move in the middle of the night in an effort to avoid public attention.

As luck would have it, a severe snowstorm moved into the area. To prevent the convoy from being held up, the Kelloggs gave the movers a key to an already rented house in Traverse City so that their belongings could be moved, should they be late in arriving. Held up by the storm south of Marquette, the Kelloggs had to spend the night in a motel. When they finally arrived at their destination, they found that the movers had already off-loaded their precious cargo. After checking the cargo list, they found certain things missing, including the two sealed crates of silver specimens. After a losing argument with the movers, the Kelloggs' start of a new life, quickly turned sour.

The Copper Country refused to give up on punishing the Kellogg family, for a short time after they purchased a new home, a law officer served them with court papers, charging them with what was known at that time, as a "Dram Shop Suit." As a result, all bank accounts of the Kelloggs were frozen by the court until the case was resolved. They were forced to hire an attorney to represent them against a party who claimed that he had been served in the tavern and was later involved in an accident. Fortunately the claimant had just enlisted in the military, so Dick called the recruitment officer whom the claimant had signed up with and told him the story. Having access to the claimant's enlistment papers, the officer said, "If he was injured in an automobile accident as he claimed, then he would have lied under oath when he signed a document that stated he was free of any on-going injuries."

Within a week after Dick contacted the recruiting officer, all charges and claims against him were dropped.

The Final Chapter

On May 5,1975, while my wife was in Arizona visiting relatives, a male stranger paid me a visit. It was late evening when I answered the door. A well dressed middle-aged man introduced himself and said that he was interested in buying my house. Without even seeing it, he offered me a price that was beyond reality. After I invited him in and showed him through the house, we sat in the finished-off basement area and discussed the possible sale of my home. When he noticed the many papers and pictures of the mine in my downstairs den, he asked me if I was a writer. When I told him I was writing a book on a lost silver mine that had been discovered by a friend of mine, he seemed overly interested. I recall that moment well, for when he briefly mentioned the Copper Country without my ever mentioning it in our conversation, I knew something was wrong.

After I told him that I couldn't commit to his generous offer until my wife returned from Arizona, he seemed oddly upset. After he left, I had the powerful feeling that something was very wrong with his unannounced visit.

A few hours later, in the middle of the night while my two sons and I slept, I was awakened by my faithful dog and found my house in flames. Fortunately, we all escaped without loss of life or injury, but part of my

INCIDENT REPORT

ELMWOOD TWP

FIRE DEPT.

☒ PHONE ☐ RADIO		BOX NO.		TIME 1:00 ☒ A.M. ☐ P.M.	DATE 3/4/75	
☐ VERBAL ☐ ADT						

COMPANY RESPONDING: *Elmwood 4 Truck - G.T. Pad I pumpkin*
CO. NO. TYPE: *Cedar Pumper - Red 8 Tanker*

TIME ARRIVED 2:10	TIME DISMISSED 6:15	HOURS 4	MILES TRAVELED 8

INCIDENT	☒ FIRE	☐ PUBLIC SERVICE
	☐ RESCUE	☐ OTHER:

LOCATION OR STREET ADDRESS: *Bay View Estates - Canton Rd.*

TYPE OF BUILDING: *Wood Structure*

OWNER: *Richard Kellogg*	OCCUPIED BY 3

BUILDING USED FOR: *Living*	SPREAD TO OTHER BUILDINGS ☐ YES ☒ NO

ORIGIN OF FIRE *Basement in Couch.*	CAUSE *Cigar -*

EXTINGUISHED BY: ☐ BOOSTER ☐ EXTINGUISHER ☒ PUMPER 3 ☐ SPRINKLER
☐ HYDRANT(S) ☐ CHEMICALS ☐ FOG ☐ OTHER: *2 Tanker*

NO. HYDRANTS USED	HOURS PUMPER WORKED 4	NO. OF LINES USED 9

MATERIAL IGNITED: TYPE *Plastic Couch.*	FORM

REASON FOR FIRE SPREADING: ☐ NON FIRE STOP WALLS ☐ OPEN STAIRS ☐ POOR WATER SUPPLY
☐ OPEN SHAFTS ☐ TYPE OF FUEL ☐ OTHER:

FORCEABLE ENTRY: ☒ DOOR ☐ WINDOW ☐ ROOF ☐ OTHER
VENTILATION: ☐ DOOR ☒ WINDOW's ☐ ROOF ☐ OTHER

FIRE DISCOVERER:
NAME: *Richard Kellogg* ADDRESS: *Canton Rd*

COMMENTS: *Visitor Left Cigar in Ash Tray. Arm of Couch.*

WITNESSES: NAME	ADDRESS
NAME	ADDRESS

INSURANCE AGENT: *State Farm* (QUARTER) INSURANCE AMOUNT

	DEATHS (NO.) INJURIES (NO.) 1

ESTIMATED VALUE:	BUILDING	CONTENTS	EQUIPMENT
ESTIMATED FIRE LOSS:	BUILDING	CONTENTS	EQUIPMENT

SPECIAL NOTES: *Fire was in Basement Had Trouble getting down to Source of Fire Divided of To much to Locate.*

SIGNATURE OF OFFICER IN CHARGE

TRAFAGRAPH SYSTEMS - P.O. BOX 1188 - NASHUA, N.H. 03060   FORM FD58

001

The Final Chapter

home was totally destroyed along with all my documents and the journals that I needed to write my story on the Wall of Silver. An investigation by the Fire Marshall revealed that the fire had started in a sleeper couch located in the finished-off basement area. Coincidentally it was the same couch that my mysterious visitor had sat on only a few hours before the fire began.

Haunted by thoughts of the mine, and the gold that it contained, I was driven to see if I could still locate it without being caught.

In mid-September 1980, looking much like a dropout of the sixties with my full beard and uncut hair, I packed my things into my new Chevrolet and headed north. Some several hundred miles later, after crossing the Portage Canal Bridge, I checked into a motel under an assumed name.

The next morning, after breakfast, dressed in clothes that blended in with the local gentry, I made the rounds checking all the bars to see if Pinnelli was still around. As I passed through the nearby abandoned small mining towns that bordered the highway, it was as though time had stood still. Nothing had really changed. When I left the highway and turned onto Cliff Drive and saw the towering cliffs come into view, a powerful fear overtook me.

Aware that the Cliff View Tavern was just across from the cliffs and offered a good view of all the traffic that entered Cliff Drive from the north, I rented a cabin next to the tavern.

From my rented cabin, I made a short trip to the Eagle River Court House to visit the Register of Deeds. It was there, from filed records, I learned that Universal Oil Products, the company that had purchased Calumet Mining Company when I owned the tavern, had since leased the Cliff Mining Company land to Homestake Mining.

Wall of Silver

I further learned that the property was leased by Homestake for a twenty-year period and that the lease would expire in 1999. For two nights I watched the entrance to Cliff Drive and noticed that a mine security patrol checked out the area about every three hours.

Unlike the night I had gone to the mine with Jake, I didn't have the advantage of an incoming storm.

On the next night, shortly after 1 a.m., when the mine patrol left the Cliff Mine property and headed north, I left my cabin and waited in the shadows. Shortly after the Cliff View Tavern closed for the night and the last vehicle had left the parking lot, I placed duct tape over my taillights to avoid being detected from the rear. Already dressed in my gear for going underground, I left the cabin, turned onto Cliff Drive and headed south. When I reached the same logging road where Jake and I parked on the night of the storm, I left the vehicle and started hiking to the mine. When I heard the sound of voices in the still night, I froze in my tracks. I recall that the moon was so bright I didn't need to use my flashlight. A closer look for the origin of the voices revealed a parked logging truck and a campfire with four men seated around it enjoying a cookout and drinking beer.

Disappointed, I returned to the cabin, packed my things, and left for home. When I returned home I was plagued with severe bouts of angina pectoris that forced me to see a heart specialist. His diagnosis was that I needed heart surgery as soon as possible. After bypass surgery, I knew my chances of returning to the mine were virtually impossible. Then on the day of Homestake Mining Company's lease running out in 1999, I again took up the cause of trying to tell the world of Jake Stockard's discovery. In the process of going over past

The Final Chapter

company records of Universal Oil Products, I learned that the Cliff Region property had been purchased by International Paper.

On April 28, 2002, I sent a registered letter to John Dillon, the CEO of International Paper, informing him that a rich uncharted silver mine was found on his company's property in Michigan's Keweenaw Peninsula, and that its discovery would change history as it is presently written. I further notified Mr. Dillon that twenty years had passed since Homestake Mining Company had leased the land and that it was subject to the possibility of abandonment under Act 554.291 of Michigan. Along with my letter, I sent Mr. Dillon the first three chapters of my book "Wall of Silver."

When I didn't hear back from Mr. Dillon, I called his secretary, who informed me that my letter along with the three chapters of my book had been sent to Atlanta, Georgia to International Paper's Land Division. When I called that division, I was further told that they passed on all the information to International Paper's Mineral Division in Houston, Texas.

Determined to elicit some sort of action, I contacted the head of the Mineral Division, Raymond Kaczorowski, by registered mail. When I failed to hear from him, I contacted Mr. Kaczorowski by phone.

When I told him that I needed a legal document that would allow me both ingress and egress to and from the described property, he appeared very willing to issue me a prospector's permit for the cost of thirty dollars. During our conversation he suggested that we meet, possibly in Lansing, Michigan, where he was expected to attend a business meeting.

Unfortunately, I never heard from Mr. Kaczorowski again.

Proof that the letter to Mr. Kaczorowski was mailed and received by the Mineral Division of International Paper.

In September of 2002, I made what would be my last visit to the Cliff Region of the Keweenaw Peninsula. Following more than thirty years since I last visited the mine with Jake Stockard, I barely recognized the region. After making numerous trips north and south on Cliff Drive, I finally found the marker I was looking for. I found the entrance to the logging road, barely visible.

The Final Chapter

Since I had contacted International Paper, large boulders had been moved into place blocking access to the mine's location.

If you are an adventurer, much like I was in my youth, don't hesitate in trying to obtain a prospector's permit to allow you legal access to the area. The mine's entrance is concealed to blend in with nature, but with the use of smoke to detect the draft coming from underground you might get surprisingly lucky. If you do gain access to the mine, you'll find a pair of dog tags from World War II lying next to the wire rim glasses. My advice, should you find the mine, is to contact The National Geographic Society and discuss the possibility of a documentary being made.

Epilogue

This is what happened to the two bags of gold that the author received from Jake Stockard for writing this book:

Shortly after I moved to Traverse City, Michigan, from the Upper Peninsula of Michigan, I tried to sell the two bags of gold coins. Unfortunately, no one in the rare coin business would buy them. The reason I couldn't sell them was because at that point in time it was against the law for a private citizen to hold gold as it was still classified as being a monetary metal.

For nearly two years I tried to sell the gold without opening the sealed bags. Then one day I received a phone call from a downstate precious metals dealer who said he'd make me a deal.

After a thorough examination of the bags (without opening them) revealed that their contents were authentic and a deal was made.

At that point in time silver was on the move. A trade was proposed. I was offered ten $1000 bags of silver

Wall of Silver

dollars based on the going price of silver per ounce for my two unopened bags of gold. I took the offer and never looked back.

As it turned out the trade was good for me, for the price of silver had reached a high of $54 dollars per ounce shortly thereafter, before it plummeted to $10.80 per ounce.

Supporting
Documents

Supporting Documents

Richard Kellogg
2837 N. Thomas Place
Traverse City, MI 49686
231-933-4662

April 28, 2002

CEO/John Dillion
International Paper
400 Atlantic Street, 15th Floor
Stanford, CT 06921

Subject: A rich, unchartered silver mine has been found on your companies property
in the Keeweenaw Peninsula of Michigan. Its discovery will change history as it is
presently written.

Dear Sir

Before I issue a press release to the media, I thought it best that I contact you regarding your mineral rights in that region. Records of the property where the mine is located indicate that more than twenty years have passed since Homestake Mining
Company leased it from International Paper. I have enclosed a copy of the abandonment act 554.291 of Michigan. My concern is whether the mine will be safe from
some renegade mining company if it is found.

To fill you in on this discovery, I have enclosed the first three chapters of my novel
"Wall of Silver" for your reading.

Respectfully yours,

Richard Kellogg

Wall of Silver

Raymond Kaczorowski / Manager
Mineral Division
International Paper
Houston, Texas 77210

Subject: So that I may conduct a legal search for the lost mine that is located

within, Township 58 North-Range 31 West within sections 28 and 29

I need the following:

Dear Ray,

On my last visit to the above described property on May 30th, 2002, I found the
needed marker that will lead me to a close proximity of the mine, but before I go any
further, I must have a document of record from your office that gives me both Ingress and
egress to the above described property without any liability on your part.

I further need from your office in writing such guarantees that if I find the mine and
retrieve a steel box containing precious coins that I get to keep the coins in exchange for
giving your company the location of the lost mine.

P.S. I might note that I intend to donate the contents within that box to my favorite
Charity

Your immediate attention to this matter will be greatly appreciated.

Respectfully Yours,

Richard Kellogg

**Subscribed and sworn
before me, a Notary Public**

Notary Signature *Rosemary M. Morley*

ROSEMARY M. MORLEY, Notary Public
Grand Traverse County, Michigan
My Commission Expires: 05-10-04

162

EAGLES ($10.00 GOLD PIECES)

	Quan. Minted	VF-20	EF-40	AU-50	MS-60	Proof-63
1878CC	3,244	$3,250	$7,000	$16,000	$32,000	
1878S	26,100	375.00	650.00	1,850	12,000	
1879	(30) 384,770	225.00	250.00	325.00	500.00	$20,000
1879CC	1,762	5,500	10,000	21,000	36,000	
1879O	1,500	2,000	4,250	9,000	22,500	
1879S	224,000	225.00	250.00	300.00	900.00	
1880	(36) 1,644,876	225.00	250.00	275.00	300.00	18,000
1880CC	11,190	400.00	700.00	1,500	8,000	
1880O	9,200	325.00	600.00	1,200	7,250	
1880S	506,250	225.00	250.00	275.00	300.00	
1881	(40) 3,877,260	200.00	225.00	240.00	285.00	19,000
1881CC	24,015	375.00	550.00	1,100	5,200	
1881O	8,350	325.00	650.00	1,100	5,000	
1881S	970,000	200.00	225.00	240.00	285.00	
1882	(40) 2,324,480	200.00	225.00	240.00	285.00	18,500
1882CC	6,764	525.00	1,000	3,000	11,000	
1882O	10,820	285.00	550.00	1,300	5,000	
1882S	132,000	220.00	245.00	285.00	500.00	
1883	(40) 208,740	210.00	225.00	250.00	285.00	20,000
1883CC	12,000	400.00	650.00	2,250	10,000	
1883O	800	2,500	6,500	10,500	28,500	
1883S	38,000	200.00	225.00	240.00	800.00	
1884	(45) 76,905	200.00	235.00	250.00	600.00	26,000
1884CC	9,925	450.00	1,000	2,600	10,000	
1884S	124,250	210.00	230.00	275.00	550.00	
1885	(65) 253,527	200.00	225.00	240.00	325.00	17,000
1885S	228,000	200.00	225.00	240.00	285.00	
1886	(60) 236,160	200.00	225.00	240.00	310.00	16,000
1886S	826,000	200.00	225.00	240.00	285.00	
1887	(80) 53,680	200.00	225.00	275.00	700.00	15,000
1887S	817,000	200.00	225.00	240.00	285.00	
1888	(75) 132,996	200.00	225.00	275.00	575.00	14,000
1888O	21,335	200.00	250.00	300.00	500.00	
1888S	648,700	200.00	225.00	240.00	285.00	
1889	(45) 4,485	250.00	350.00	800.00	2,000	18,000
1889S	425,400	200.00	225.00	240.00	285.00	
1890	(63) 58,043	200.00	225.00	275.00	600.00	15,000
1890CC	17,500	300.00	425.00	625.00	1,700	
1891	(48) 91,868	200.00	240.00	265.00	310.00	12,000
1891CC	103,732	275.00	350.00	500.00	800.00	
1892	(72) 797,552	200.00	230.00	240.00	285.00	13,500
1892CC	40,000	325.00	450.00	700.00	2,850	
1892O	28,688	200.00	230.00	275.00	400.00	
1892S	115,500	225.00	245.00	275.00	350.00	
1893	(55) 1,840,895	225.00	245.00	275.00	285.00	13,500
1893CC	14,000	350.00	625.00	1,600	4,500	
1893O	17,000	225.00	250.00	300.00	600.00	
1893S	141,350	225.00	250.00	275.00	400.00	
1894	(43) 2,470,778	200.00	225.00	240.00	285.00	13,500
1894O	107,500	200.00	225.00	300.00	850.00	
1894S	25,000	200.00	250.00	700.00	3,200	
1895	(56) 567,826	200.00	225.00	240.00	285.00	12,000
1895O	98,000	225.00	250.00	300.00	500.00	
1895S	49,000	225.00	235.00	650.00	2,350	
1896	(78) 76,348	200.00	225.00	240.00	285.00	12,000
1896S	123,750	225.00	275.00	550.00	2,350	
1897	(69) 1,000,159	200.00	225.00	240.00	285.00	12,000

Because Jake Stockard gave Dick Kellogg two mint sealed bags of ten dollar gold coins that were dated 1890, there is no way of knowing what the mint dates are of the three thousand coins that remain in the mine. The above chart will show the possible dates and values of those coins once they have been found.

163

Wall of Silver

The value of the consideration for this instrument is less than $100 and this instrument is exempt from real estate transfer tax by reason of M.S.A. 57.456(5)(a).

QUITCLAIM DEED

THIS INDENTURE, made by Henley Holdings, Inc., a Delaware corporation, with its principal office at Liberty Lane, Hampton, New Hampshire 03842 , "Grantor", and Lake Superior Land Company, a Delaware corporation, with its principal office at 101 Red Jacket Road, Calumet, Michigan 49913, "Grantee".

WITNESSETH, that Grantor for and in consideration of the sum of Ten and no/100 Dollars ($10.00) to it in hand paid by Grantee, the receipt whereof is hereby confessed and acknowledged, does by these presents alien, release, remise, convey and quitclaim unto Grantee all that certain piece or parcel of land situated in the County of Keweenaw and State of Michigan, known and described in Exhibit A attached to this deed.

IN WITNESS WHEREOF, Grantor has caused these presents to be signed by Robert P. Grasseschi, its Vice President, and countersigned by Robert L. Melroy, its Assistant Secretary, and its corporate seal to be hereto affixed this 1st day of January, 1987.

HENLEY HOLDINGS, INC.

By _[signature]_
Robert P. Grasseschi, Vice President

In the presence of:

Shelley Lazarus
Witness Shelley Lazarus

B. J. Clancy
Witness B. J. Clancy

Countersigned:

[signature]
Robert L. Melroy, Assistant Secretary

STATE OF ILLINOIS   )
) ss.
COUNTY OF COOK   )

Personally came before me this 1st day of January, 1987, Robert P. Grasseschi, Vice President, and Robert L. Melroy, Assistant Secretary of the above named corporation, to me known to be such Vice President and Assistant Secretary of said corporation, and acknowledged that they executed the foregoing instrument as such officers as the deed of said corporation by its authority.

Patricia H. Trimarco
Notary Public

This instrument was drafted by:

Robert L. Melroy
Suite 490
2340 S. Arlington Heights Road
Arlington Heights, Illinois 60005

> "OFFICIAL SEAL"
> PATRICIA H. TRIMARCO
> Notary Public, State of Illinois
> My Commission Expires Oct. 15, 1990

Quitclaim Deed page 1

Supporting Documents

EXHIBIT A

In Section 25:

   N½   (containing 320.00 acres more or less)
   S½   (containing 320.00 acres more or less)

In Section 26:

   N½ (containing 320.00 acres more or less)

In Section 27:

   N½ (containing 320.00 acres more or less)

In Section 28:

   Entire Section (containing 640.00 acres more or less)

In Section 29:

   Entire Section (containing 640.00 acres more or less)

In Section 30:

   Entire Fractional (containing 621.98 acres more or less)

In Section 31:

   Entire Fractional except a parcel of 10.37 acres in S½ of S½ as
   described in Liber Y of Deeds, Page 416-417, Keweenaw County
   records, and a parcel of 9.93 acres in the SW¼ of SW¼ as described
   in Liber Y of Deeds, Page 477 of Keweenaw County Records
   (containing 597.48 acres more or less)

In Section 32:

   NE¼   (containing 160.00 acres more or less)
   E½ of NW¼ (containing 80.00 acres more or less)

In Section 33:

   E½   (containing 320.00 acres more or less)
   W½ of NW¼ (containing 80.00 acres more or less)

In Section 36:

   E½   (containing 320.00 acres more or less)
   W½   (containing 320.00 acres more or less)

IN TOWNSHIP 58 NORTH, RANGE 31 WEST:

In Section 1:

   S½ (containing 320.00 acres more or less)

In Section 2:

   S½ of SE¼ (containing 80.00 acres more or less)

In Section 10:

   NE¼ of SE¼ (containing 40.00 acres more or less)
   S½ of SE¼ (containing 80.00 acres more or less)

In Section 11:

   Entire Section (containing 640.00 acres more or less)

In Section 12:

   Entire Section (containing 640.00 acres more or less)

Quitclaim Deed page 2

Wall of Silver

In Section 13:

Entire Section (containing 640.00 acres more or less)

In Section 14:

Entire Section except a parcel of land in W½ of NW¼ of said Section 14, T58N-R31W, described as follows: Beginning at a point on the West boundary line of Section 14, 1371.47 feet South of the NW corner of said Section 14; thence run N 66° 48' E a distance of 404.28 feet; thence S 23° 12' E a distance of 245 feet to a point on the Northerly right-of-way line of Highway M-26 as now established; thence Southwesterly along said Northerly right-of-way line 503 feet to a point on the West boundary line of Section 14; thence North along said Section line 217.59 feet to the Point of Beginning, containing 2.362 acres more or less (containing 637.64 acres more or less)

In Section 15:

NE¼ (containing 160.00 acres more or less)
NE¼ of NW¼ (containing 40.00 acres more or less)
S½ of NW¼ (containing 80.00 acres more or less)
S½ (containing 320.00 acres more or less)

In Section 16:

Entire Fractional except all that part of Gov't. Lot 1 which lies Northerly of the cneterline of M-26, containing 23.1 acres more or less and except 16.2 acres in the recorded Plat of Eagle River East (containing 479.2 acres more or less)

In Section 17:

Entire Fractional except 126.2 acres in Plat of Eagle River East (containing 263.6 acres more or less)

In Section 18:

Entire Section except that portion therein of the Village of Eagle River, containing 4.79 acres and except 128.8 acres in the recorded Plat of Eagle River East; and except part of parcel recorded in Liber 6 of Deeds, Page 91, Keweenaw County Records which lies North of Section line between Sections 18 and 19 containing 0.26 acres more or less (containing 52.90 acres more or less)

Town of Eagle River:

Lots 1, 2, 3, 4, 5, 6 & 7, Block 2 (containing .77 acres more or less)
Lots 2, 3, 4, 5 & 6, Block 3 (containing .56 acres more or less)

In Section 19:

Entire Section except that portion of the Village of Eagle River in NW¼, 57.43 acres; also except the following described parcel of land: Commencing at the NE corner of Block 24 in the Village of Eagle River; thence Northeasterly along a prolongation of the Southeasterly boundary of Fourth Street 60 feet to a point on the Northeasterly boundary of Maple Street, said point being on the Northeasterly boundary of the Village of Eagle River, since a portion of said Village was vacated June 22, 1860. Beginning at said point, thence Northeasterly along a prolongation of the Southeasterly boundary of Fourth Street 200 feet; thence at a right angle Southeasterly 120 feet; thence at a right angle Southwesterly 200 feet; thence at a right angle Northwesterly 120 feet to the place of beginning, containing 0.55 acres; and except part of parcel recorded in Liber 6 of Deeds, Page 91, Keweenaw County Records, which lies South of the section line between Sections 18 and 19, containing 23.30 acres; and except 8.8 acres in the recorded Plat of Eagle River East (containing 502.68 acres more or less)

Quitclaim Deed page 3

166

Supporting Documents

In Section 19, cont'd.:

Town of Eagle River:

All that part or parcel of land situated in the Town of Eagle
River, Keweenaw County, described as follows: Commencing at
the Northwest corner of Store owned by John Senter & Company,
said point being on the Easterly boundary of East Main Street in
the Town of Eagle River as laid down on a plat of said Town,
recorded in the office of the Register of Deeds of Keweenaw
County; thence run Northerly along the Easterly boundary of
said East Main Street to a point on the Southerly line of Front
Street; thence run Northeasterly along the Southerly line of
Front Street to the Easterly line of a purchase made by said
Senter of the Phoenix Copper Company by deed dated September 17,
1850; thence North 20 West along said line of said purchase to
the Northerly line of Front Street; thence Easterly along the
Northerly line of Front Street to the Southerly corner of Lot 4,
Block 1; thence Northerly on the line between Lots 4 and 5 in
Block 1 to the shore of Lake Superior; thence Southwesterly
along the lake shore to the meander corner on the town line between Ranges 31 and 32 West. Commencing again at said Northwesterly corner of said store; thence Westerly along the line
of said store 83 links; thence S 43° 6' W to said range line;
thence North on the range line to said meander corner, being
Lots 1, 2, 3 and 4 of Block 1 and Lots 1, 2 and part of Lot 3
(River Lots) at Mouth of River, also part of Block 9
(containing 1.46 acres more or less)

Fractional (Surface only) Block 9 (containing .14 acres more or
less)

Lot 7 (Surface only), Block 21 (containing .27 acres more or less)

In Section 20:

Entire Section except W½ of NW¼ of SW¼ (containing 620.00 acres more
or less)

In Section 21:

Entire Section (containing 640.00 acres more or less)

In Section 22:

NE¼ (containing 160.00 acres more or less)
S½ (containing 320.00 acres more or less)

In Section 23:

Entire Section (containing 640.00 acres more or less)

In Section 24:

Entire Section (containing 640.00 acres more or less)

In Section 25:

Entire Section (containing 640.00 acres more or less)

In Section 26:

Entire Section (containing 640.00 acres more or less)

In Section 27:

Entire Section (containing 640.00 acres more or less)

In Section 28:

Entire Section (containing 640.00 acres more or less)

Quitclaim Deed page 4

Wall of Silver

In Section 29:

    E½ (containing 320.00 acres more or less)
    W½ (containing 320.00 acres more or less)

In Section 30:

    Entire Fractional (containing 601.18 acres more or less)

In Section 31:

    NE¼ of NE¼ (containing 40.00 acres more or less)
    S½ of NE¼ (containing 80.00 acres more or less)
    NW¼ of NW¼ (containing 31.13 acres more or less)
    SE¼ of NW¼ (containing 40.00 acres more or less)
    S½ Fractional (containing 301.80 acres more or less)

In Section 32:

    Entire Section (containing 640.00 acres more or less)

In Section 33:

    N½ of NE¼ (containing 80.00 acres more or less)
    SE¼ of SW¼ (containing 40.00 acres more or less)
    S½ of SE¼ (containing 80.00 acres more or less)

In Section 34:

    NW¼ (containing 160.00 acres more or less)
    S½ (containing 320.00 acres more or less)

In Section 35:

    NE¼ (containing 160.00 acres more or less)
    S½ (containing 320.00 acres more or less)

In Section 36:

    Entire Section (containing 640.00 acres more or less)

IN TOWNSHIP 58 NORTH, RANGE 32 WEST:

In Section 24:

    Lot 1 (less Houghton Monument desc.) (containing 52.15 acres more or less)
    Lot 2 (containing 60.20 acres more or less)
    Lot 3 (containing 29.85 acres more or less)
    Lot 4 (containing 44.50 acres more or less)
    SE¼ of SW¼ (containing 40.00 acres more or less)
    E½ of SE¼ less 1.11 acres Cemetery (containing 78.89 acres more or less)
    SW¼ of SE¼ (containing 40.00 acres more or less)

In Section 25:

    Entire Section (containing 640.00 acres more or less)

In Section 27:

    Entire Fractional, less 0.78 acres sold to Keweenaw County recorded
    in Liber 4 of Deeds, Page 103, Keweenaw County Records and except
    60.1 acres in recorded Plat of Five Mile Point East (containing 285.92
    acres more or less)

In Section 28:

    Lot 1, less 21.65 acres S.H. Lths. (containing 40.00 acres more or less)
    Lot 2, less 16.40 acres S.H. Lths. (containing 40.00 acres more or less)
    Lot 3, less 3.6 acres S.H. Lths. (containing 30.80 acres more or less)

29 -

4/71

Quitclaim Deed page 5

Supporting Documents

Received for Record the 20th day of July A.D. 1972 at 11:30 A.M.

[signature]

Register of Deeds

SHORT FORM OF AGREEMENT

THIS AGREEMENTS, dated as of the 7th day of July, 1972, by and between HOMESTAKE MINING COMPANY, a California corporation ("Homestake"), and UNIVERSAL OIL PRODUCTS COMPANY, a Delaware corporation ("UOP"),

WITNESSETH:

IN CONSIDERATION of Ten Dollars ($10.00), paid by Homestake to UOP, the receipt of which is hereby acknowledged, and in further consideration of the mutual covenants, agreements, and promises herein contained, the parties hereto agree as follows:

ARTICLE I

OPTION TO LEASE MINING PROPERTY

1.1 **Grant of Option.**

   (a) UOP hereby grants to Homestake the sole and exclusive option to lease the Mining Property (hereinafter called the Option) upon the terms and conditions hereinafter set forth.

   (b) "Mining Property" means the property more particularly described in Exhibit A attached hereto and incorporated by reference herein.

   (c) Homestake may exercise the Option by giving notice in writing to UOP of its intention to so do at any time during the term of the Option or any extension thereof provided that Homestake shall have fully satisfied the conditions precedent enumerated in Section 1.4 of the Agreement mentioned in Section 3.1 hereof.

1.2 **Term of Option.**

   (a) The Option hereby granted shall be for a term of one hundred twenty (120) days from the date of execution of the Agreement mentioned in Section 3.1 hereof. This initial one hundred twenty (120) day period shall hereafter be referred to as "Phase I".

   (b) Homestake may extend the Option for an additional period of one hundred twenty (120) days from the end of Phase I in the manner provided in the Agreement mentioned in Section 3.1 hereof. This second one hundred twenty (120) day period shall hereafter be referred to as "Phase II".

   (c) Homestake may extend the Option for an additional period of six (6) months either from the end of Phase I or from the end of Phase II in the manner provided in the Agreement mentioned in Section 3.1 hereof. This six (6) month period shall hereafter be referred to as "Phase III". If by the end of Phase I or Phase II, as the case may be, Homestake has not obtained all permits necessary to commence dewatering of the Centennial No. 6 workings, Phase III shall continue until six (6) months after the date Homestake has obtained all permits necessary to commence such dewatering, provided, however, that any and all such permits must have been obtained within one (1) year after commencement of Phase III.

   (d) Homestake may, at any time during Phase I, Phase II, or Phase III extend the Option for an additional period of three (3) years from the end of Phase I, Phase II or Phase III, as the case may be, in the manner provided in the Agreement mentioned in Section 3.1 hereof. This three (3) year period shall hereafter be referred to as "Phase IV".

   (e) Homestake may extend the Option for three (3) additional period of one (1) year each from the end of Phase IV in the manner provided in the Agreement mentioned in Section 3.1 hereof. The three (3) one (1) year extensions shall hereafter be collectively referred to as "Phase V".

   (f) In no event shall any force majeure extend the Option for a longer period than eleven (11) years from the date the Agreement mentioned in Section 3.1 hereof is executed.

ARTICLE II

LEASE OF MINING PROPERTY

2.1 **Lease.** UOP hereby agrees to lease the Mining Property to Homestake, effective upon the date of Homestake's exercise of the Option in accordance with the provisions of the Agreement mentioned in Section 3.1 hereof.

2.2 **Term of Lease.** The term of the Lease of the Mining Property shall be for sixty (60) years from the date of Homestake's exercise of the Option and shall continue thereafter for the term of the economic life of the Mining Property.

2.3 **Exclusive Possession.** Homestake shall have the exclusive and peaceable possession and quiet enjoyment of the Mining Property and the right to explore and mine the same during the term of this Lease.

ARTICLE III

agreement

3.1 This Short Form of Agreement is executed for the purpose of affording notice of the existence of an Agreement dated as of the 7th day of July, 1972, by and between the parties hereto, and of the terms and provisions thereof, which terms and provisions are incorporated herein by reference for all purposes. A copy of said Agreement is on file in the respective offices of Homestake and UOP and may be inspected by all proper parties.

3.2 This Shore Form shall not limit, decrease, increase, or in any manner affect any of the terms of said Agreement or any rights, interests, or obligations of the parties thereunder.

Executed this 12th day of July, 1972, in Des Plaines, State of Illinois.

Short Form of Agreement page 1

✕ 169

Wall of Silver

EXHIBIT A
'mining property'

Part I - Mineral Rights

UOP does hereby let and lease, as hereinafter described in Part I, unto Homestake all of UOP's right, title and interest in and to any and all ores, metals and minerals in, upon or under the premises located in Keweenaw and Houghton Counties, Michigan, which are broadly described in Exhibits A-1 and A-2, attached hereto and incorporated by reference herein. The descriptions on Exhibit A-1 constitute Class I mineral rights. The descriptions on Exhibit A-2 constitute Class II mineral rights. Homestake shall have free and unrestricted access to Class I mineral property in accordance with the terms of this Agreement, but shall have no rights to Class II mineral property unless anduntil UOP grants Homestake permission to include such Class II mineral rights, or any part thereof, as a Class I mineral right. Homestake may request such permission from UOP at any time during the term of this Agreement. UOP will grant such permission, unless the particular Class II area is needed or desired by UOP for any reason other than mineral exploration and/or development.

Part II - Surface Rights

To the extent of its right, title and interest, UOP does hereby grant to Homestake the right to use so much of the surface of Class I mineral rights, and so much of the surface of Class II mineral rights to which UOP has granted Homestake permission as hereinabove mentioned in Part I, as may be required for the conduct of mineral exploration and/or development thereon. Homestake shall notify UOP of its intention to make use of the surface of the Mining Property as provided herein. Such notice shall specify each separate parcel which is to be used and the time at which such use will begin, which time shall not be sooner than thirty (30) days from the date of such notice.

Part III - Legal Descriptions

It is understood that the description listed on Exhibits A-1 and A-2 are broad in nature and that UOP shall supply Homestake with complete legal descriptions of the areas listed on Exhibits A-1 and A-2. UOP hereby undertakes to furnish such particular legal descriptions by the end of Phase I. In the event UOP does not furnish Homestake with such descriptions by the end of Phase I, then Phase I shall continue until such time as such descriptions are furnished.

Part IV - Claims

UOP hereby represents that to the best of its information, knowledge and belief, that there is no known litigation, dispute, or claim bearing adversely on UOP's title to the Mining Property.

Part V - Additions to Legal Descriptions

UOP and Homestake recognize that there are certain areas not listed in Exhibits A-1 and A-2 which, to the extent of UOP's right, title, and inteest, if any, are properly includable under this Agreement. When the complete legal descriptions referred to in Part III hereof are completed they will include to the extent of UOP's right, title and interest, if any, Class I and Class II mineral rights, as the case may be, in the following sections:

Short Form of Agreement page 2

Supporting Documents

Township 55 North, Range 33 West, Houghton County - Section 10

Township 56 North, Range 33 West, Houghton County - Sections 2, 18

Township 57 North, Range 33 West, Keweenaw County - Section 28, 32.

Township 54 North, Range 32 West, Houghton County - Sections 21, 29, 33.

Township 55 North, Range 32 West, Houghton County - Sections 1, 13, 15, 22, 23, 27, 35.

Township 56 North, Range 32 West, Houghton County - Sections 2, 10, 12, 14, 23, 24, 25, 26, 33, 35.

Township 57 North, Range 32 West, Keweenaw County - Sections 7, 10, 27, 29, 34, 36.

Township 55 North, Range 31 West, Houghton County - Sections 7, 17.

CLASS II

Township 56 North, Range 31 West, Keweenaw County - Sections 15, 17, 19, 21, 23, 27, 29, 31, 32, 33.

Township 57 North, Range 31 West, Keweenaw County - Sections 23, 27, 32.

Township 56 North, Range 30 West, Keweenaw County - Section 5.

Township 57 North, Range 30 West, Keweenaw County - Sections 25, 33.

EXHIBIT A-1
" CLASS I MINERAL RIGHTS"

Section	Township North	Range West	County
1 through 36	53	33	Houghton
1 through 36	54	33	Houghton
3 through 9, 16 through 22, 28 through 33	55	33	Houghton
1, 3, 9 through 17 19 through 36	56	33	Houghton
2 through 10, 15 through 21, 24 through 25, 29 through 31, 35 through 36	57	33	Keweenaw
S½ = S ¼ of 18	53	32	Houghton
2 through 10, 13, 16 through 20 23 through 26, 30 through 32, 35 through 36	54	32	Houghton
2 through 4 9 through 12, 14, 16, 21, 24 through 26, 28, 31 through 34, 36	55	32	Houghton
1, 3 through 9, 11, 13, 15 through 22, 27 through 32, 34, 36	56	32	Houghton
1 through 5 8 through 9, 11 through 26, 28, 30 through 33, 35	57	32	Houghton
25, 35, 36	58	32	Keweenaw
5 through 6, 8, 18 through 19, N1/2 of 20	55	31	Houghton

Short Form of Agreement page 3

⚒ 171

Wall of Silver

Short Form of Agreement page 4

172

Supporting Documents

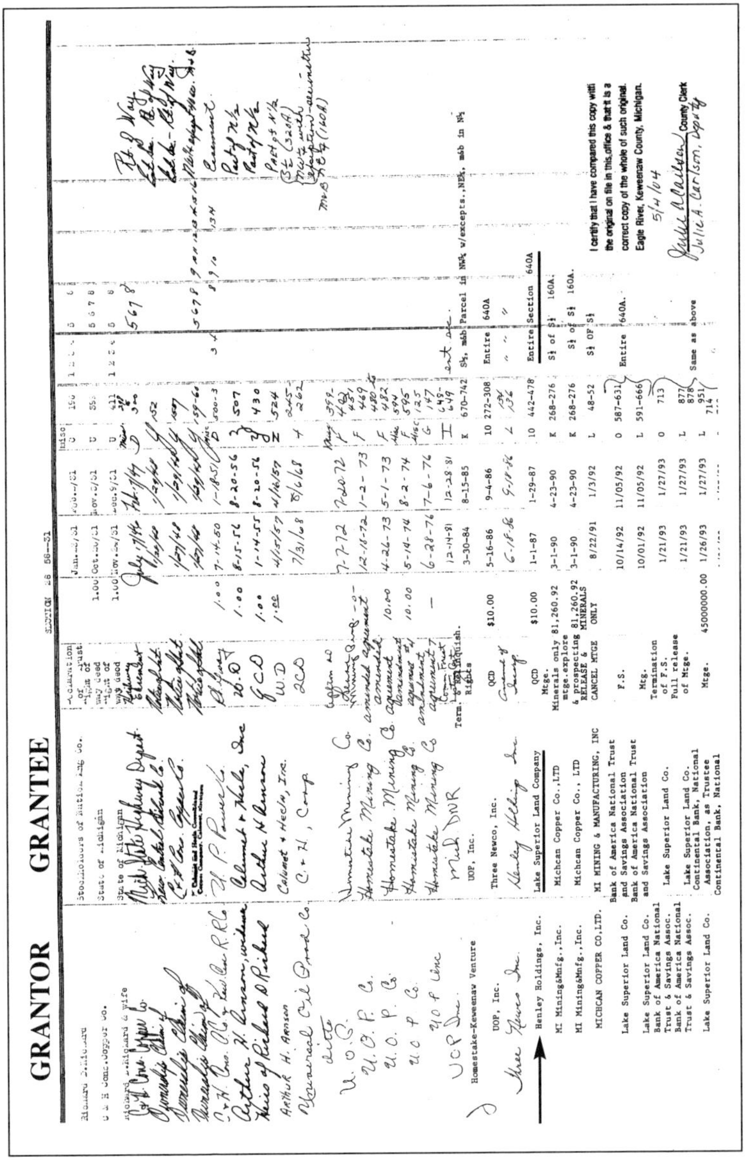

A document register (rotated sideways) with columns **GRANTOR** and **GRANTEE** and handwritten entries largely illegible.

Partial legible grantee/grantor entries include:
- Stockholders of Native Lig. Co. — State of Michigan
- Three Mexco, Inc.
- DOP, Inc.
- Henley Holdings, Inc. — Lake Superior Land Company
- MI Mining&Mfg.,Inc. — Michgan Copper Co.,LTD
- MI Mining&Mfg.,Inc. — Michgan Copper Co. LTD
- MICHIGAN COPPER CO.LTD. — MI MINING & MANUFACTURING, INC
- Lake Superior Land Co. — Bank of America National Trust and Savings Association
- Bank of America National Trust & Savings Assoc. — Lake Superior Land Co.
- Bank of America National Trust & Savings Assoc. — Continental Bank, National Association, as Trustee
- Lake Superior Land Co. — Continental Bank, National

About The Author

Richard Kellogg
The Author

In his youth Richard Kellogg survived the skies over Europe with the Eighth Air Force. After a career as a design engineer and inventor, Richard retired early from public life. To satisfy his love of the outdoors he moved to Upper Michigan's Keweenaw Peninsula, where he purchased a famous tavern. This is where the discovery of the "Wall of Silver" took place.

Avery Color Studios, Inc. has a full line of Great Lakes oriented books, puzzles, cookbooks, shipwreck and lighthouse maps, lighthouse posters and Fresnel lens model.

For a full color catalog call:
1-800-722-9925

Avery Color Studios, Inc. products are available at gift shops and bookstores throughout the Great Lakes region.